108 課綱、全民英檢中級適用

英語 *Make Me High* 系列

漢堡式大考英文段落寫作
Paragraph Writing: Easy as a Hamburger （二版）

林君美

· 學歷

國立臺灣大學外國語文學系學士
美國哈佛大學教育研究所碩士

· 經歷

臺北市立建國高級中學英文教師

三民書局

序

英語 Make Me High 系列的理想在於超越，在於創新。

這是時代的精神，也是我們出版的動力；

這是教育的目的，也是我們進步的執著。

針對英語的全球化與未來的升學趨勢，

我們設計了一系列適合普高、技高學生的英語學習書籍。

面對英語，不會徬徨不再迷惘，學習的心徹底沸騰，

心情好 High ！

實戰模擬，掌握先機知己知彼，百戰不殆決勝未來，

分數更 High ！

選擇優質的英語學習書籍，才能激發學習的強烈動機；

興趣盎然便不會畏懼艱難，自信心要自己大聲說出來。

本書如良師指引循循善誘，如益友相互鼓勵攜手成長。

展書輕閱，你將發現……

學習英語原來也可以這麼 High ！

給讀者的話

　　一個色彩豐富鮮豔、口感甜美紮實的漢堡人人都愛。而一個英文段落應該也是如此的外表誘人、內容充實。本書「漢堡式大考英文段落寫作」的目的在於用最精簡、有趣的方式，協助國內即將升大學的同學，使其能在很短的時間內，對英文段落寫作有清楚的觀念；並經由有效的練習，寫好大學學科能力測驗等大考的英文作文考題。

　　本書共分九章。第一章「評分樣例」，旨在幫助初學者了解一篇好的英文段落式作文應有的樣貌。第二章「段落的組成」及第三章「找文思及擬大綱」，是要讓同學了解下筆前要做的準備。第四章「主題句」、第五章「支持句」及第六章「結論句」則是在幫同學練好寫作的基礎功。第七章「統一性、連貫性及緊密連接」及第八章「避免常見錯誤」是筆者在批改同學作文練習時最常看到的弱點，也是同學要將分數提高不可或缺的進階觀念與練習。最後的第九章「寫作範例及練習」，則提供近年常出現考題的佳作供同學參考，文後附有類似題型供同學練習。

　　為求文風的多元與趣味，筆者避免採用由老師撰寫的文章。本書蒐羅許多段落練習及範文，其中許多篇文章為筆者的學生在就讀臺北市立建國中學高三時所撰寫的好作品，再經筆者與外籍編者稍加潤飾而成，其中不乏在正式學測等大考中得到18、19分的佳作重現。在此感謝96學年度高三尤俊凱、吳健揚、吳善加、林欣聖、林俊佑、胡思彥、唐葆真、陳冠豪、陳昱中、陳韋豪、張耕榜、梁立明、賀星晧、楊涵傑、蔡毅昕、黃奕翔、黃彥霖、曾介平、蘇育成及97學年度高三陳怡仁、黃威棣、葉重如慷慨提供範文供全國的學弟妹們觀摩。

　　用餐愉快！

林君美 mei

TABLE OF CONTENTS

Chapter 1 ▶ Grading Samples
評分樣例 1

Chapter 2 ▶ The Structure of a Paragraph
段落的組成 11

Chapter 3 ▶ Generating Ideas and Making an Outline
找文思及擬大綱 15

Chapter 4 ▶ The Topic Sentence
主題句 21

Chapter 5 ▶ The Supporting Sentences
支持句 31

Chapter 6 ▶ The Concluding Sentence
結論句 39

Chapter 7 ▶ Unity, Coherence, and Cohesiveness
統一性、連貫性及緊密連接 47

Chapter 8 ▶ Avoiding Common Errors
避免常見錯誤 63

Chapter 9 ▶ Writing Samples and Exercises
寫作範例及練習 83

Key ▶ 解答 107

✕ Acknowledgments ···

◆ 本書收錄的歷年試題著作權屬財團法人大學入學考試中心基金會
   所有,轉載請註明出處。

◆ 本書圖片來源:Shutterstock

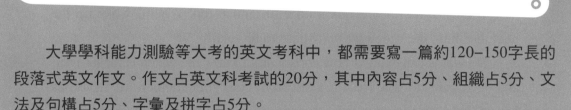

Chapter 1

Grading Samples
評分樣例

大學學科能力測驗等大考的英文考科中，都需要寫一篇約120–150字長的段落式英文作文。作文占英文科考試的20分，其中內容占5分、組織占5分、文法及句構占5分、字彙及拼字占5分。

在熟悉段落寫作各種該注意的事項之前，相信同學一定很想知道，學測等大考英文作文該長什麼樣子？到底哪樣的文章可以在大考中得高分？因此在第一章中，我們特別請同學就兩種大考英文作文題目撰寫短文，挑出從優到劣各五篇，以大考中心公布的英文作文評分指標加以評分並加註評語，以提供同學一個基本概念，並預估自己的成績。

1.1 An Apology Letter to a Friend

說明： 1. 依提示在「答案卷」上寫一篇英文作文。

2. 文長120個單詞(words)左右。

提示： 你(英文名字必須假設為George或Mary)向朋友(英文名字必須假設為Adam或Eve)借了一件相當珍貴的物品，但不慎遺失，一時又買不到替代品。請寫一封信，第一段說明物品遺失的經過，第二段則表達歉意並提出可能的解決方案。

請注意： 為避免評分困擾，請使用上述提示的George或Mary在信末署名，<u>不得使用自己真實的中文或英文姓名</u>。(97年學測)

1

Dear Adam:

Last week when I was troubled by having nothing to fit my suit, you lent me your watch without any hesitation. If it were not for its elegant design, I couldn't have won so much admiration. I had a lot of fun at the party, and maybe I had drunk a little too much too. When I woke up the next morning, the watch was nowhere to be seen!

No words can express how sorry I am. I know the watch is meaningful and memorable to you, for it is a gift from your grandmother. My heart has been filled with regret, which has tortured me day and night since I made the stupid and unforgivable mistake. I have visited dozens' of department stores to find an identical watch, but in vain. Though I can't return you a watch as precious as the original one, the same company now has the latest production, with which I wish I could remedy my fault. I know I can never undo the mistake. Still, I hope you can accept my sincere apology. Will you forgive me and take me as your best friend as in the past?

Yours truly,

George

說明： 主題明確，內容敘述相當具體且完整。重點分明，組織具連貫性。句型富變化，幾無文法錯誤(第二段第四句dozens' 應為dozens)。詞彙使用妥適。

內　容 (5 分)	組　織 (5 分)	文法、句構 (5 分)	字彙、拼字 (5 分)	總　分 (20 分)
5	5	4.5	4.5	19

Dear Eve:

I'm sorry to tell you that I lost the watch you lent me when I went hiking yesterday. I was walking in the bamboo forest when a shiny green snake lept down from a branch and charged toward me. Frightened, I turned and ran as fast as I could. Luckily, it didn't come behind me, but I felt the watch slipped off my wrist while I was running. Then, I headed back with great caution to find it, but saw the snake again! This time it wasn't interested in me, instead, it slid away looking surprisingly satisfied. Bewildered, I heard a soft ticking sound coming from the snake's stomach as it disappeared into the woods. Then I finally understood—it swallowed the watch!

I feel deeply sorry, for I know the watch was a birthday present from your grandma and therefore was very meaningful to you. Still, I have to thank you for lending it to me, because in a strange way it actually saved my life from that horrible snake. Let me make it up to you. Next week, I'll take you to the department store and buy you a new watch. Or maybe, if you would like to, we can go hiking again and look for your watch. Perhaps the snake throwed up and left it somewhere. Above all, I really hope you could forgive me.

Sincerely your's, George.

Aug. 13. 2018

說明：主題敘述具體，情節稍嫌誇張但能自圓其說。句型變化豐富且運用得宜，偶有文法錯誤(第二段倒數第二句的throwed up應為had thrown up)，未正確斷句或未使用連接詞連接子句。用字適切，雖偶有用法與拼字錯誤(第一段第二句的lept應為leapt；結尾問候語應為Sincerely Yours；George應在下一行並與Sincerely對齊；日期應該在信件的最右上角等)，但未影響文意之表達。標點符號稍有不當。

內　容 (5 分)	組　織 (5 分)	文法、句構 (5 分)	字彙、拼字 (5 分)	總　分 (20 分)
4	4	3.5	3.5	15

Dear Adam,

　　Do you remember the trip to Kenting I told you yesterday? It was so great but I found your notebook left with my full memory there just now. I surfed the Internet then play music with your notebook every night there before I sleep. I love the songs so I turned it on all night. But the last morning in Kenting, I packed the packages with the lively loop. And then, I forgot your note book on the bed there! I am so sorry about that. But I can't afford to buy one back to you so soon. I'll try my best to save money to compensate you. Although my notebook is not that multi-function as yours, it's still work. May you use mine temporarily? I'll give it back to you as soon as possible. Again, I'm so sorry about that.

Sincerely, George

說明：內容尚稱切題，但相關敘述發展不全，部分句子語意不清楚。組織不夠連貫。文法及拼字錯誤，影響部分文意之表達；標點使用稍有不當。沒有依照提示文分兩段，另扣一分。

內　容 (5 分)	組　織 (5 分)	文法、句構 (5 分)	字彙、拼字 (5 分)	總　分 (20 分)
3.5	3.5	3	3	12

4

Eve:

To my apology, I lost the pearl necklace which you lended me last week at a wedding bouguet. I put it in a case with a lock on it. When I checked the case the next day there wasn't anything inside. I had asked the restaurand but in vain.

I am so sorry for my careless and I should have watched out this precious necklace. There is two alternatives that I can think of to solve this problem. if you like you can tell me how much it is and I will pay the money back to you. if you don't like then I will have to ask you where did you get that necklace, and I will buy it back to you. At the last, I want to apologize against for my mindless.

Sincerely yours,

George

說明： 雖有主題，但相關敘述未能發展；不但文法錯誤多，用字、拼字錯誤亦多，嚴重影響文意之表達。

內 容 (5 分)	組 織 (5 分)	文法、句構 (5 分)	字彙、拼字 (5 分)	總 分 (20 分)
2.5	2	1.5	1.5	7.5

5

Dear Eve,

Can you still remember the last sunday that you I have borrowed a swatch from you? this wednesday when I were taking the Taxi, when I were in a hurry, So when I arrived the destination, I ran down the Taxi, and I can't find my watch everwhere!, I think it must lost Somewhere in the Taxi.

I'm vary sorry for losing your Swatch, which your mother gave it to you. I think it's very expensive, I can't afford to buy a new one now. Therefore, can you wait for several month, when I save enough money, I'll buy a new one for you.

Your best friend, George

說明： 內容太少，段落發展無章法。因文法、用字、拼字錯誤多，大小寫、標點亦混亂，嚴重影響文意之表達。字數不足，另扣一分。

內 容 (5 分)	組 織 (5 分)	文法、句構 (5 分)	字彙、拼字 (5 分)	總 分 (20 分)
1	1	1	1	3

1.2 An Impressive Advertisement

說明： 1. 依提示在「答案卷」上寫一篇英文作文。
2. 文長至少120個單詞。

提示： 廣告在我們生活中隨處可見。請寫一篇大約120–150字的短文，介紹一則令你印象深刻的電視或平面廣告。第一段描述該廣告的內容(如：主題、故事情節、音樂、畫面等)，第二段說明該廣告令你印象深刻的原因。(97年指考)

1

Of all the advertisements I have ever seen, the one that impressed me most was seen in a magazine. In this advertisement, lots of bottles were filled with water melted from a huge iceberg and later became the bottled waters we drink everyday.

On first seeing the advertisement, I thought the bottled waters were the products to sell and the melting iceberg was there to give us an image of how pure and clean the water was. But as I took a closer look, a slogan came into my eyes, saying "Stop drinking bottled waters", which followed by a series of numbers telling me how many pollutants were gave off to the environment during the process of producing and delivering these things I drink every day. It was not until then that I realized I was destroying our planet by taking up the habit of buying and drinking bottled waters all the time. The shocking fact made me decide to change. Now wherever I go, I take an empty bottle with me and fill it whenever I feel like quenching my thirst. Being able to do our planet a small favor can be really satisfying. In my case, this advertisement is not only impressive but also extremely successful.

說明： 主題清楚、具體，內容豐富具啟發性；重點分明、組織完整且連貫。文句結構變化豐富，文法錯誤很少且無礙文句流暢(但第一段最後everyday應分為2字every day；第一段第二句的bottled waters應該沒有s；第二段第二句的were gave off應該為were given off；廣告用語結束的逗點應該在引號裡面)；用字得宜(但第二段第二個字first為贅字)。

內 容 （5分）	組 織 （5分）	文法、句構 （5分）	字彙、拼字 （5分）	總 分 （20分）
5	5	4.5	4.5	19

2

At the bottom of the ninth inning, Chih-Yang is at the third base, Chen-Ming is at the second base. The batter, Tsai-Feng-Ang, turns his head to search for the coach's hint...no, he's looking at that bowl of Dr. Kang Instant Noodles! He's thinking, if he hits a goodbye-homerun, Chih-Yang will come back first and eat that egg, and Chen-Ming will eat all the noodles after that. The only way he can enjoy that bowl of Dr. Kang Instant Noodles himself is to be struck out. It is three balls and two strikes. The pitcher suddenly pitches the ball, and it is a walk! Now the three players can't even drink the soup!

This commercial is really interesting, especially for those who watch baseball. Chih-Yang, Chen-Ming, and Feng-Ang are the best three players in the Brother Elephants, the baseball team with most fans in the Chinese Professional Baseball League. The commercial first tells you that this was a tight game and now it was the most important part of the game. Every player would try to do his best at this time, but Fen-Ang didn't. Instead, he was looking for a strike out, just because of a bowl of instant noodles! In the end, he got a walk and had to go onto the first base, so he couldn't even drink the soup. The commercial shows how good the noodles taste by this way, which is very creative, and that's the main reason I think this commercial is interesting. Moreover, I love watching baseball!

說明： 主題清楚，敘述發展完整且緊湊風趣。然而第二段有些句子重複性高，使得文章稍嫌冗長。有些句子談論自己對棒球的熱愛有離題之嫌。另外人名的大小寫、連字號、及時態偶有錯誤。

內 容 (5 分)	組 織 (5 分)	文法、句構 (5 分)	字彙、拼字 (5 分)	總 分 (20 分)
4.5	4	3.5	3	15

3

Lights shine through the pure color of the whisky, looking at the field full of weats, aftered by the process of making whisky. It's a commercial of a name brand whisky. Their main title is "Never have we been our opponent's opponent, in fact, we are our opponent's guide line."

What a bluddging attitude! Some may even marked it as egoism, but I think it's an interesting philosophy. When your goal is to beat your opponents, you and your opponents are on the same level, but when you set to be their guide line, it's a whole different thing. I'd rather regard this kind of attitude as self-esteem, or self confidence, it's a trust to your own ability. That's why this commercial impressed so much.

說明： 內容雖提及與主題相關之事物，但未能就主題充分發揮。多處語意不清楚，尤其第一句幾乎無法理解。文法、用字、拼字錯誤多，句子與句子中間沒有正確斷句或連接，明顯影響文意之表達。

內 容 （5 分）	組 織 （5 分）	文法、句構 （5 分）	字彙、拼字 （5 分）	總 分 （20 分）
2.5	2.5	1.5	1.5	8

4

There was a television advertising which made me with deep impression. It was about a conversation of two men. "Who are you?" the young man asked. And the old man that has serious bald answer "I am you in the future." "How come. I can't believe it." And Then, their produce show on the.

why did it affect me so much? Because when I washed my head every times. there were many pieces of hair fell on the ground. I was afraid that I will be like the man

說明： 雖有主題，但相關敘述未能發展；不但文法錯誤多，用字、拼字、大小寫、標點錯誤亦多，嚴重影響文意之表達；字數不足，另扣一分。

內 容 (5分)	組 織 (5分)	文法、句構 (5分)	字彙、拼字 (5分)	總 分 (20分)
2	2	1	1	5

5

There are various of interesting advertisements on TV. And the funny advertisements are my favorite. For example, Many young man play football with many old man. Old men are very powerful, and young men are very weak. They play the funny game, and drink beverage together. The advertisement's subject is beverage.

The have many funny

說明： 內容太少，段落發展全無章法。文法、用字、拼字錯誤多，嚴重影響文意之表達。字數不足，另扣一分。

內 容 (5分)	組 織 (5分)	文法、句構 (4分)	字彙、拼字 (4分)	總 分 (20分)
1	1	0.5	0.5	2

漢堡祕方 高分作文的特點：

1. 內容豐富完整，組織有邏輯連貫。
2. 每一個句子都與主題密切相關，沒有句子離題。
3. 句型、用字有變化且使用正確。
4. 文法、拼字錯誤少。
5. 字數略超過所規定的120字，大概在150–180字之間。

CHAPTER 2

The Structure of a Paragraph

段落的組成

同學可能還沒有寫過英文段落,不過一定有吃過漢堡。有趣的是,段落的組成與漢堡的組成非常相似。漢堡由上層麵包、中間餡料,與下層麵包組成,並有美乃滋增加潤滑口感;而段落則是由主題句、支持句與結論句組成,並藉由統一性、邏輯連貫及緊密連接等技巧使文章流暢。

漢堡的組成與段落的組成

STRUCTURE OF A HAMBURGER	STRUCTURE OF A PARAGRAPH
富含芝麻香氣的上層麵包	針對主題定一個主題句 (topic sentence)。
新鮮的生菜和番茄 香濃的起司 鮮嫩多汁的牛肉	以主題句為中心寫下相關的支持句(supporting sentences)。
紮實的下層麵包	呼應主題句,總結支持句的發展方向寫下結論句(concluding sentence)。
美乃滋	• 統一性 (unity) 　每一個句子都契合主題。 • 連貫性 (coherence) 　句子的編排具邏輯連貫性。 • 緊密連接 (cohesiveness) 　用轉承詞來連接句子與句子、善用同義字與代名詞。

 **ACTIVITY** 請閱讀以下文章，並分別標示出topic sentence、supporting sentences和concluding sentence。

The Most Unforgettable Family Activity

Once my family and I went hiking at night. That was a beautiful evening and the moon was shining. The scenery and natural sounds made us relaxed. After we arrived at the top of the hill, we started to eat moon cakes and chat. My father talked to us about life. It was the most wonderful and unforgettable family activity to me.

請再閱讀改寫過的文章，並分別標示出topic sentence、supporting sentences和concluding sentence。

The Most Unforgettable Family Activity

On the Mid-Autumn Festival last year, my family and I went hiking at night to appreciate the beauty of the moon. We went to Elephant Hill near my house. On our way to the top of the mountain, we saw moonlight shining on trees. We could hear cicadas buzzing around us. These beautiful scenes and delightful sounds made my family and I relaxed and happy, though we were panting after having hiked for a while.

Arriving at the top of Elephant Hill, we could see a majestic and silver moon hanging in the night sky. Its beauty was beyond description. On the top of the hill, my family and I ate moon cakes and shot the breeze. Then my father taught me a lesson about life. He said, "Just as the moon waxes and wanes, so life has its ups and downs. But looking on the bright side of life will help you go through most of the difficulties." What Father said that night has had a lifelong effect on me. This hiking trip has been the most impressive and meaningful family activity I have ever had.

漢堡祕方　因為以下幾個特點，使得修改後的文章比原來內容更豐富，結構
也更完整：‧‧‧‧‧‧‧‧‧‧‧‧‧‧‧‧‧‧‧‧‧‧‧‧‧‧‧‧‧‧‧‧‧‧‧‧‧‧

1. 主題句清楚點出文章主題。
2. 支持句的數量比較多，也比較具體，能充分說明主題。
3. 結論句總結段落文意。
4. 善用轉承詞將句子與句子緊密連接。

Note ✏️

CHAPTER 3

Generating Ideas and Making an Outline

找文思及擬大綱

同學常常會問，構思和寫大綱很重要嗎？考試的時間都不夠了，怎麼會有時間擬大綱？

想像一位店員在做漢堡前，一定要先知道客人點了什麼漢堡，並根據客人的點餐，在心裡先決定這個漢堡的麵包、內餡材料、醬料是什麼，然後動手去做。如果客人點了牛肉漢堡，可不能只放起司、忘了放牛肉就送餐；如果客人點米漢堡，也不能擅自改成麵包。另外，各種材料的分量要適中分配，放了太多肉、缺了生菜也不美味。

看到了作文的題目也是如此。在著手寫之前，要先找文思並規劃出一個大綱，行文時根據大綱發展，才能將作文寫得內容豐富、組織嚴謹。如果同學寫了一句才開始想下一句要寫什麼，很可能寫出散亂離題的文章，字數也難以控制，往往更浪費時間。因此考試的時候，能迅速地擬一個簡潔扼要的大綱，對於控制時間及掌握文章組織是很有幫助的。

3.1 用5W1H法則找文思

尋找文思的方式有好幾種，像是腦力激盪法、畫枝狀圖，或自由寫作；但是最簡單、最省時、最適合大學入學考試的方法就是針對題目提出人、事、時、地、物等問題，並寫下答案的關鍵字。這些問題是以Who、What、When、Where、Why、How這六個疑問詞開始的問句，我們稱為5W1H法則。

以作文題目An Unforgettable Trip為例，我們可以利用5W1H來尋找文思的問題有：

5W1H問題	回答關鍵字
Who did I go with? **Who** did I meet?	my classmates pedestrians and other bikers
What happened?	a bike tour around Taiwan
When did the event happen?	this summer
Where did I go?	tour the island, clockwise
Why was it unforgettable?	sweltering hot, tiring, but met friendly people
How did I feel about the trip?	unforgettable

3.2 擬大綱──從關鍵字找出較易發揮的三點

　　利用5W1H來尋找到文思之後，就可以著手擬大綱了。在寫作文前擬一份簡潔的大綱，不僅能夠幫助同學有組織地呈現文章的要點，更能避免離題或組織鬆散。擬大綱的時候，只需寫下關鍵的單字或片語，以節省時間。

大綱製作方法：

　　以An Unforgettable Trip為例，首先從5W1H找到的文思之中，挑出自己覺得容易發揮的三點，訂出排列順序，如依照時間順序安排、空間順序安排，或依最重要排到最不重要，用關鍵字擬出簡單的大綱。一般寫作經常在接近結尾處帶入高潮，但在考試時先提最精采之點，也可吸引閱卷老師的注意，提高印象分數。

段落大綱範例：

TOPIC SENTENCE	did something extraordinary, planned a bicycle tour
SUPPORTING SENTENCES	1. fascinating scenery and delicious food 2. cheers from pedestrians and other bikers 3. met friendly and hospitable people
CONCLUDING SENTENCE	etched in my heart forever

漢堡祕方 ••

1. 建議同學大考時拿到試卷，先看作文題目為何，用5W1H法則找文思，擬定一個由關鍵字組成的簡單大綱。

2. 接著寫選擇題，過程中如果還想到什麼好點子，也可以記在考卷的末頁。

3. 最後留下至少30–40分鐘寫翻譯及作文。

••

ACTIVITY 1 請閱讀下面的文章，並分別標示出topic sentence、supporting sentences和concluding sentence。

An Unforgettable Trip

Yearning to do something extraordinary while young, my classmates and I planned a bicycle tour around Taiwan this summer. We decided to travel around the island clockwise in twelve days. After making all the arrangements and practicing several times, we set out on our adventure.

The weather was swelteringly hot every day, even the breezes felt like fire. Shortly after departure each morning, we were soaked in sweat. Nevertheless, the torture of the heat, the soreness in our legs, and the exhaustion of our energy were all rewarded by the fascinating scenery and delicious food along the road. Moreover, we were greeted by the loud cheers from pedestrians and other bikers. Like magic, we always seemed refueled and rode faster with the cheers. Once, two of our bikes got flat tires, and a few passers-by lent us a helping hand without hesitation. Meeting so many friendly and hospitable people around the island was indeed heartwarming.

Overall, I felt lucky to have joined this tour, which tested my physical and mental strength, broadened my horizons, and cemented the friendship with my classmates. This memory will be etched in my heart forever, and I will always cherish this amazing experience.

 **2** 請以An Embarrassing Experience為題，構思題材並且擬出
大綱。

1. 找文思

5W1H問題	回答關鍵字
Who was there?	
What happened?	
When was the event?	
Where did it happen?	
Why was it embarrassing?	
How did I feel about the experience?	

2. 擬大綱──從上方關鍵字中找出較易發揮的三點

TOPIC SENTENCE	
SUPPORTING SENTENCES	1. 2. 3.
CONCLUDING SENTENCE	

3. 發展成文章

Note ✏️

CHAPTER 4

The Topic Sentence

主題句

4.1 主題句的定義

　　英文作文與中文作文有一個很不同的地方，就是英文作文裡的各個段落都會有一個中心思想，而它通常出現在第一句或非常接近開頭的地方，點出文章主題及作者的立場，我們稱之為主題句。

　　主題句就像漢堡的上層麵包，有濃濃的芝麻香氣，抹上奶油，烤得香酥又柔軟，令人第一眼就食慾大開。雖然專業作家寫出的文章或報導不見得有明顯的主題句，但是對剛開始學習英文寫作的同學來說，將主題句放在段落的開頭，能使讀者或閱卷老師一目了然，更可避免發展文章時離題；而最重要的好處，就是有助在評分項目中的組織部分(占5分)得到高分。

 ACTIVITY *1* 請將下面段落中的主題句畫底線。

1

The Most Unforgettable Family Activity

　　The most unforgettable experience I had with my family happened last year, when my parents and I went to Mt. Ali to see the beautiful sunrise.

　　In order to see the sunrise, we woke up at around 2 a.m., putting ourselves together for the challenge ahead. After hitting the road, the three of us started our journey with great excitement. At first, I found the road not too steep, so I could still chat with my mom without losing my breath. As we climbed higher, the journey became more arduous. I started to feel tired and cold, saying that I wanted to give up, for the goal seemed unreachable. At that time, my parents told me that only with determination and perseverance could a man be

successful, insisting that I keep going. Motivated, I carried on the journey and reached the goal eventually.

Now every time I face obstacles, I reminisce about this trip, for I know these obstacles will be gone as long as I stick to my dreams and never give up. In the end, the breathtaking view of sunrise will be my reward.

The Thing I Regret Most

Whenever I recall the incident which happened two years ago, I regret not having done the right thing at the right time. It took place on my way home on a bus. There being an English test the following day, I took the only empty seat on the bus and started memorizing vocabulary. About ten minutes later, an old lady carrying several grocery bags stepped on the bus. Since there were no more seats, the old lady put her belongings down and stood on the shaky bus. While I was expecting to see someone yield his or her seat, the old lady fell, with her things scattered everywhere and one leg hurt. I joined other passengers to help pick her things up and called for an ambulance, but I still felt deeply sorry. If I had yielded my seat to the old lady right after she got on the bus, the accident could have been prevented. After this experience, I decided to be the first one to yield my seat to anyone who really needs it.

4.2 寫主題句時應該注意的事項

明確(definite)而不含糊(not vague)

- We should do something to protect our environment.   **✗** vague
- To protect our environment, first we should conserve energy.   **O** definite

具體(specific)而不可太廣泛(not too broad)

- I go to a high school in Taipei. **✗** broad
- My school, located in downtown Taipei, is a learning paradise. **O** specific

具有可討論性(discussible)而非僅陳述事實(not a fact)

· Taipei is the capital city of Taiwan.   (**X**) fact
· Taipei is the cultural, financial, and political center of Taiwan.   (**O**) discussible

簡潔(concise)而不冗長(not lengthy)

· Nothing broadens one's horizons as travel.   (**O**) concise
· The proverb "Traveling a thousand miles is better than reading ten thousand books" means that we can learn more by traveling than by reading.   (**X**) lengthy

多用主動語氣(active voice)避免被動語氣(avoid passive voice)

· The present my grandmother left me will always be cherished by me.   (**X**) passive
· I will always cherish the present my grandmother left me.   (**O**) active

ACTIVITY 2 請挑出較佳的主題句並說明原因。

1 _____

   A. There are 23 million people in Taiwan.

   B. Taiwan, a small island, is a densely populated country.

2 _____

   A. Jake adores his brand new Mercedes-Benz.

   B. Jake likes his car.

3 _____

   A. Today I am going to tell you about my English teacher.

   B. There is no one else funnier than my English teacher.

4 _____

   A. My favorite movie, *The Terminal*, is both entertaining and inspiring.

   B. My favorite movie whose name is *The Terminal* is both entertaining and inspiring because it has great characters and a brilliant story plot.

5 _____

   A. The day my house collapsed in the earthquake will never be forgotten by me.

   B. I will never forget the day my house collapsed in the earthquake.

4.3 常見的主題句寫法

　　主題句的內容應該包含文章的主題(topic)並提示段落發展方向(controlling idea)。寫主題句的方法有很多，主要目的是引起讀者對內文的好奇心。在學測等大考的短篇作文中，較適合的方法有提出驚人的事實、引用名言、引述統計數字、提問法及陳述立場等。

1. 提出驚人的事實(Striking Fact)

Nature Is Our Best Teacher

　　Believe it or not, spider silk is stronger than steel. Steel is indeed a fine artificial substance, a proof of human's amazing technology. Yet, it still fails to compete with spider silk, a substance made by spiders, which many people despise. As a result, the fact that there is much we can learn from nature is self-evident.

　　If we research on spider silk thoroughly, we may figure out why spider silk can be strong as well as light, and then apply its features to the production of bullet-proof vests. Some of human's inventions are also inspired by nature. Sonar technology, which is inspired by dolphins, is a good example.

　　However, we human beings, who consider ourselves the cleverest creatures, don't learn from nature like we used to do. Instead, we are destroying it. Not only do we devastate the environment we live in, but also waste precious learning resources. We should be humble and learn from nature so we can keep improving and making our lives better. Next time when you are amazed by the awe-inspiring Taipei 101, don't forget the little spider on that strong web in the tree next to it!

說明： 在文章的開頭點出一個科學事實，那就是柔軟的蜘蛛絲比鋼更強韌，一般人可能很難相信這個事實，作者便善用此驚人的事實，說服讀者相信自然的偉大力量。

2. 引用名言(Quotation)

Drink Moderately

To drink or not to drink, that is the question. As we know, drunk driving is responsible for a large percentage of car accidents and traffic fatalities. We often hear of someone doing something embarrassing or even committing crimes after a drinking bout. However, we also know that drinking is inevitable in many social occasions and it is quite a good leisure activity. Some researchers even indicate that some kinds of wine are good for health. Therefore, should we drink or not?

As far as I am concerned, the question is not whether we should drink or not, but how we drink. First, we should not drink and drive. By doing so, we can easily lower the possibilities of car accidents. Second, we should know how much we can drink and don't drink beyond that limit to control our behavior. If we know the right way of drinking, it will be a good hobby instead of a fatal one. Drinking is good as long as we drink moderately!

說明：在莎士比亞悲劇《哈姆雷特》的對白中，主角的臺詞To be or not to be, that is the question. 人人琅琅上口。在這裡作者運用巧思，將名句改寫，並應用在喝酒與不喝酒的困難選擇上，引起讀者的興趣，加深讀者的印象。

3. 引述統計數字(Citing Statistics)

Wildlife Conservation in My Hometown

Located in Taipei are one national park, at least three nature reserves and more than one hundred hiking trails, making this city not only a home for us but also a shelter for all kinds of creatures. The Yangmingshan National Park is famous for its volcanic terrain and it also houses the largest population of the Formosan Blue Magpie(臺灣藍鵲), the city bird of Taipei. The bird is one of the many species indigenous to Taiwan. It's guaranteed that you can't find them anywhere else on earth. Moreover, due to the diversity of habitats and the unique geographical location, Taipei is ideal for migratory birds. For example, the well-known Guandu Nature Park provides an enormous area of wetland habitat for hundreds of species of migratory birds each year, making it one of the best bird-watching spots on the island. These symbolize Taipei's efforts in wildlife conservation.

說明：主題句中用one national park、at least three nature reserves和more than one hundred hiking trails等數字，來點出臺北豐富的生態資源，增加文章的說服力。

4. 提問法(Raising a Question)

Taroko Gorge, Nature's Masterpiece

Do you know which scenic spot in Taiwan is most visited by foreign tourists? It is ranked high among all gorges around the world and known as Taiwan's Grand Canyon. You must have figured what I am talking about. Right! It is Taroko Gorge, nature's masterpiece. Situated in the tranquil and beautiful town of Hualien, Taroko Gorge is formed mainly by the erosion of Liwu River. Therefore, cliffs, valleys, rivers, and waterfalls are all its famous features.

Breathtaking cliffs and valleys can be seen everywhere in Taroko Gorge. Standing in the midst of the mountains and watching the steep cliffs reaching into the sky, you will definitely be awed by the almighty power of nature. Waterfalls are also the places you shouldn't miss. Standing near them, you will feel the cool breeze caressing your face and the water galloping like thousands of horses. It will certainly be an unforgettable experience.

Taroko Gorge is a place where you can see beautiful mountains and water at the same time. Come to Taroko Gorge and experience how it feels like to be embraced by nature!

說明：本篇的一開始提出一個問題，一般人可能不知道它的答案，作者藉由回答問題帶出主題句，以引起讀者想知道答案的好奇心，進而引領讀者閱讀下文，更加了解這個美麗的景點。

5. 陳述立場(Stating Standpoints)

What Does Taiwan Need Most Now?

Taiwan, a beautiful island, is abundant in natural resources. What does it still need? I think the answer is conscience. Not only celebrities but also ordinary people lack it. One can see people on the streets telling lies, not yielding their seats to the old, being indifferent to others, just to name a few. These are the evidence of the urgent need of conscience in Taiwan.

A piece of research once hit the headline. According to statistics, only one fifth of high school students would yield their seats to the old. They often pretend to be sleeping or just keep fiddling with their cellphones. A picture was put above the headline—a high school student was sitting and playing with his cellphone on the bus while an old man was standing beside. If we Taiwanese had conscience, things like this couldn't have happened. People would take action to yield seats. Taiwan then would be well-known worldwide, not only for its beautiful scenery, but for the conscience and the love people have for one another.

說明：這是一篇論說文類型的文章，作者在第一段直接表達自己的立場，認為臺灣社會最需要的是良心。之後再論述理由，說明如果人人有良心的話，臺灣的形象會更加提升。

 ACTIVITY 3 請為下面段落挑選一個主題句。

1

My Hometown

_____ Take a walk on the streets and you'll find yourself in a world of fantasy. Public artworks designed by local modern artists can be seen all over the city, making walking more than joyful.

For those who prefer something classical, the National Palace Museum may be a great choice. It houses the world's finest collections of traditional Chinese fine art. The National Theater and Concert Hall are another two fantastic choices. Situated in the C.K.S. Memorial Hall, they hold many types of performances from all over the world inside the outstanding traditional Chinese architecture.

Simultaneously, Taipei brings together ample diverse cuisines around the world. You'll have endless choices in both Asian and Western food, not to mention local snacks in night markets that visitors will never forget! And, if you are a fan of shopping, there are always a great variety of shopping malls, department stores, and open-air markets waiting for you to explore.

_____ *a. Taipei is where the headquarters of many financial and governmental institutions are located.*

_____ *b. As the capital city, Taipei is noted for its cityscape of skyscrapers and technology parks.*

_____ *c. Taipei is a city rich in art, culture, and gourmet food.*

My Hometown

    The well-known landmark Taipei 101, one of the tallest buildings all over the world, symbolizes the remarkable financial, commercial and entertainment achievements of this city. The gorgeous structure reflects the active commercial activities in Taipei. Towering to the height of 508 meters, the building stands proudly in Taipei and is recognized internationally for the first-class technology used to build it. Famous companies, such as Microsoft and Google, have already moved in, creating even more economic miracles from this futuristic skyscraper.

    In recent years, Taipei has been setting up the "technology corridor of Taipei," connecting the three Technology Parks in Neihu, Beitou and Nangang. By bringing priority industries together, this technology corridor will form the most advanced industrial area in Taipei and give us the greatest advantages over other countries.

_____ *a. Taipei is where the headquarters of many financial and governmental institutions are located.*

_____ *b. As the capital city, Taipei is noted for its cityscape of skyscrapers and technology parks.*

_____ *c. Taipei is a city rich in art, culture, and gourmet food.*

 **ACTIVITY** 4 請為下列段落補上主題句。

If I Could Invent a Product

    It would allow people to go back to the past, go to the future, or go anywhere in the present time. The time machine would be unbreakable and equipped with a sophisticated auto-navigation system, a protection shield, and defensive weapons.

    With the time machine, I could go back to ancient times to visit different heroes and places, and even uncover some great mysteries in history. I would know how the Egyptian pyramids were built, or how big the tomb of Chinese emperor Qin Shi Huang actually was. In addition, I could check out the future to see whether the global warming phenomenon has gotten any worse, or whether human beings have evolved into a new species. If the Earth were to be taken over by aliens in the future, I could protect myself with the enhanced weapons and shield in my time machine.

Time itself is a mystery. Hopefully, with my time machine, I could explore time and have a great journey.

Internet and My Life

First, playing online games really helps me relieve stress. As a student I have to take lots of exams and do tons of research, which often put me under great stress. When I feel overwhelmed, I relax myself for a while by playing games online. There is a stereotype that only bad students play online games. But the fact is, I've made some good friends to play and study together. To win a game or set a new record, it's important for us to work as a team and help each other. At school, we study together and solve problems in the same manner. Besides, playing online games also serves as a driving force urging me to learn English because most of the games are English-based. That's why I study English so hard! In sum, the Internet has many positive influences on my life.

漢堡祕方

1. 主題句應該包含文章的主題及段落中心思想。
2. 主題句應清楚、明確、可討論、簡潔，並盡量使用主動語氣。
3. 對初學者而言，主題句以放在段落的開頭為佳。可用提問法、引述驚人的事實、名言、統計數字，或表明議論的立場等五種寫法。

Note ✏️

CHAPTER 5

The Supporting Sentences
支持句

5.1 支持句的定義

　　一個段落的第一句話經常是主題句，使讀者能夠清楚地了解到整段的大意。接下來的句子是支持句，支持句就像漢堡中間夾的食材──生菜和番茄要新鮮爽口，牛肉要甜美多汁，起司要濃郁滑順，讓人一口咬下，吃到多層次的美味。而食材的挑選，當然要與漢堡的上層麵包相輔相成。

　　支持句應該針對主題句鋪陳出條理清晰的說明，或是提出足夠的事實證明主題句的陳述，亦或是描述主題進行的過程。這一部分的闡述十分重要，是不是能夠說服、感動讀者，一切仰賴這一些句子是否組織得當。

ACTIVITY *1* 請為下列主題句挑選出三個適合的支持句。

1 Topic sentence: My personal experience of learning English centers on continual practice.

Supporting sentences:

_____ a. I make it a habit to listen to the radio and read English magazines every day.

_____ b. English is the most important international language.

_____ c. With an excellent command of English, one can easily find a well-paid and fulfilling job.

_____ d. Secondly, extensive reading is one of my learning skills. From storybooks to novels, I swim in the fascinating plot in the English language.

_____ e. Finally, I enjoy listening to English songs and singing along with the melody. As I repeat the touching lyrics, I also perceive the deep meaning within.

_____ f. These habits above help me master the language.

2 <u>Topic sentence</u>: During the summer vacation before I entered high school, my whole family went on a tour of the Qingjing Farm.

<u>Supporting sentences</u>:

_____ a. Out of the window of the inn we stayed at, I saw clouds floating up from the valley, and in the distance were a few farmers collecting tea leaves diligently.

_____ b. We had never taken a trip for a long time because of my heavy schoolwork.

_____ c. Although the continuous rain forced us to stay indoors, the picturesque view of nature mixing the color of the hills with the mysterious fog was even more impressive.

_____ d. How I wish my family and I could take a trip together more often!

_____ e. What's more, the golden sunlight penetrating the thick gray clouds and spreading its joy to the green land was the most breathtaking scene I had ever seen.

_____ f. That was an unforgettable experience because I had never thought that Taiwan has such beautiful scenery in Nantou.

5.2 支持句的寫法

　　在段落寫作中，最實用的支持句寫法有舉例、描述過程或細節、用數據佐證，或分享一則小故事等。

1. 舉例(Examples)

Someone That Influenced My Life

　　My mother is a career woman. A huge part of my memory, however, is not so much her being a tough woman as a loving and caring mother. <u>She made a point of helping me discover my potential. We spent a lot of time developing different interests, such as art, music and cooking. It was not that she didn't care about my schoolwork, but that she believed one can do more than just focus on academic performance. Even though Mother worked late on most nights, she made sure I could have a homemade dinner by preparing it beforehand.</u>

To people with a career to pursue and a family to support, the balancing act is overwhelming. Yet, my mother did it with grace. She even came to my football games. Through her actions, I learned that I could have my own choice of direction in life without being bound by traditional social values. I have also learned to keep love and compassion in mind, no matter how busy I may be. I will cherish these beautiful values for life.

說明：作者視母親為影響自己生命的人。支持句詳實舉出母親教育孩子、照顧孩子飲食，並辛勞兼顧家庭與工作，種種示範影響自己的價值觀，都是在提出具體的例子以佐證主題。

2. 描述過程或細節(Details)

The Thing I Regret Most

When it comes to the thing I regret most, I cannot help but recall the conflict between my junior high classmate and me. It was a rainy day, and I was unhappy because my umbrella was broken. My classmate, Tom, was showing off his birthday gift—a watch—to others in the classroom. Out of curiosity, I stepped closer to take a look at the watch. I took the watch and examined it. But accidentally, it slipped and fell to the ground. All of us were astonished by the accident, and Tom yelled loudly at me. Feeling upset about my umbrella and the accident that had just happened, I yelled back furiously and criticized his beloved watch. Tom stared at me as if he could not believe what I had said. After a moment of silence, he took the broken watch away without saying a word. Not until a few days later did I realize that the watch was a precious gift from his late grandmother. Words could not describe how regretful I felt. If only I had been more cautious or apologized for my carelessness!

說明：作者曾經因情緒失控而做出後悔的事情，在此使用順序法描述整件事情發展的經過，將人、事、時、地、物等細節交代得很清楚。

3. 用數據佐證(Statistics)

On Drinking and Driving

One can never be too careful when driving. Road accidents are listed as one of the top ten major causes of death. Last year alone there were over two hundred cases, and that was when the drivers were sober. According to statistics, drinking and driving increases the fatality rates of car accidents by twenty five percent.

The results of drunk driving are always devastating. Therefore, it is surprising that the number of drunk driving is still on the rise, even with stricter police checks. The seriousness of the problem has prompted a search for answers in the authorities. It appears that punishments for drunk drivers were too lenient. For example, those taken into custody can retrieve their cars after paying a fine. In order to save more lives, the authorities have decided to toughen regulations and tighten the legal alcohol intake threshold for drivers. Hopefully, the new efforts will significantly curb drunk driving and make the streets safer for both pedestrians and drivers.

說明：作者提出許多數字來佐證酒後駕車的嚴重性而非空談，值得大家重視。

4. 小故事(Anecdotes)

Thinking Before Speaking

We should be cautious before speaking, for "a word spoken is past recalling," and there is no knowing what the outcome will be.

Long ago in China, a great famine gripped the land. A rich man poured out his wealth to feed the poor. One day, while he was busy distributing food, a haggard-looking woman limped by. "You, woman!" called the rich man, pointing his finger at her, "Come eat!" "I would not," she replied, turning to the rich man, "for I had been called upon as a dog." Realizing he had hurt the woman's pride, the rich man quickly apologized for his attitude. The woman was resolute, however, and starved to death.

The rich man had meant well, but his moment of disrespect had cost the woman her life. Doesn't that teach us something about thinking twice before speaking?

說明：作者藉著歷史上有名的不食嗟來食而餓死的故事，來佐證主題句所說做人要
謹言慎行、尊重他人。一個動人的故事，往往比成篇的說教更能說服讀者。

ACTIVITY 2 下面段落中已有主題句和結論句，請補上支持句。

主題句：Because of its combination of positive and negative points, the
Internet can't easily be classified as good or bad.

支持句：

_____

_____

_____

_____

_____

_____

結論句：Therefore, people must learn to choose suitable websites and spend a
proper amount of time using the Internet.

主題句：For various reasons, the Dragon Boat Festival was my favorite festival
when I was a child.

支持句：

_____

_____

_____

_____

_____

結論句：I will never forget the fun I used to have on the Dragon Boat Festival.

5.3 概括性與具體性(General and Specific)

支持句在文章中的角色是佐證或說明主題句,因此必須避免模糊的字眼,要用明確的詞語塑造鮮明的意象,這樣才能有效地傳達意念,說服或感動讀者。因此在寫支持論點時,應認識並練習使用具體而明確的詞彙和句子。

怎麼樣的詞彙屬於模糊、概括性高的(general)?而什麼詞彙比較明確具體(specific)呢?以science和chemistry為例,science涵蓋的範圍較廣,是概括性較高的字,而chemistry則較明確,因為chemistry具體說出了science中的某個特定領域。再以art和watercolor(水彩畫)為例,art比較模糊,watercolor則比較明確。在支持句中,使用chemistry或watercolor這樣具體的例子,能夠協助說服讀者。

請閱讀下方的句子,左邊的句子概括性較高,右邊的句子則比較明確,請感受看看具體的詞彙如何帶給讀者深刻的印象。

概括　General	具體　Specific
1. I love music.	I love listening to jazz. → 指出喜歡聆聽的音樂種類,而非廣泛的總稱。
2. My dad likes to nag.	My dad likes to nag about how poorly I perform at school. → 舉出了細節說明嘮叨的內容。
3. I once took a trip with my family.	I took a trip to Hualien with my family last summer. → 明確指出旅遊的時間和地點。
4. A woman sat in the front of the concert hall, watching Jacky Cheung on stage.	A well-dressed woman sat in the front of the crowded concert hall, watching Jacky Cheung singing on stage. → 在名詞前後加上描述性的詞語,使句子更明確。

ACTIVITY 3 請挑出較具體明確的句子並說明原因。

1 _____

A. My grandmother always cooks on New Year's Eve.

B. My grandmother always cooks more than 10 dishes—including chicken, fish, pork, rice cake, dumplings, etc.—on New Year's Eve.

2 _____

A. Julia is a couch potato who spends at least 10 hours a day watching TV.

B. Julia spends a lot of time watching TV.

3 _____

A. I hate going to school because of many things.

B. I hate going to school because I detest taking tests and wearing uniform.

4 _____

A. A suspicious-looking man, covered up in a black jacket and a helmet, wandered outside the bank before the robbery took place.

B. A man appeared before the robbery took place.

漢堡祕方 寫一個段落的作文會不會太長了？可不可以分段？ ················

　　大考作文題通常是引導寫作，分不分段及每段寫什麼須嚴格按照說明。若無要求，那麼把120–150字的作文寫成一段並不嫌長。如果一定要分段，可以把主題句擴展成類似開場的第一段，但最多只能寫兩三句，千萬不可占太多篇幅。支持論點和結論句就一起放在第二段。

Note

CHAPTER 6

The Concluding Sentence

結論句

6.1 結論句的定義

　　結論句就像是漢堡的下層麵包，如果上層是一般的麵包，那麼下層麵包可不能是米漢堡。下層的材質必須與上層麵包一模一樣，雖然少了芝麻但必須更厚實。沒有下層麵包緊緊地支撐著食材，漢堡可就零散不成形了。這就類似段落中的結論句，結論句通常是在段落的結尾，用來總結段落，將思路帶回主題句的主旨。

 ACTIVITY 1 請用底線標出下面段落中的結論句。

1

My Personal Hero

　　My personal hero is Kevin Lin (Lin Yi-Chieh), the number one jogger in Taiwan. As the first Asian athlete to win the championship in a super marathon, he has inspired many people in Taiwan.

　　Thin and short though Kevin looks, he conquers every difficulty he meets with his strong wills and extraordinary courage. For example, when he jogged in the Sahara Desert, he showed no fear of the violent sandstorm. He looked on the bright side and did not give up. Sometimes, so strong was the wind that he could not open his eyes or stand still. Burning hot sand gave him blisters on the feet, resulting in extreme pain. However, he insisted on completing the race despite these setbacks. He knew that only when a man makes efforts to achieve his goal can he taste the fruit of success.

　　The story of Kevin Lin tells me that I should always do my best and never give up. It is with courage and determination that Kevin makes the impossible possible and becomes a super hero in my heart.

Internet and My Life

For me, the Internet is more than search engines because it opens up a window to the world. I've always wished to visit different places and make friends from other countries. But I'm just a poor student who can go nowhere but stay at home and school. The Internet helps me fulfill my dream. Ever since I knew how to use the Internet, I often log on to websites of foreign tour offices. And that dramatically changes my life because I can virtually travel to any country I like and admire the breathtaking views. So far, I've taken wonderful tours to countries like Norway and Madagascar for free, while comfortably sitting in front of my computer and accessing information about those places. What's even more fabulous is that I've made many foreign friends in the chat rooms or on the international pen pal websites. Thanks to them, I can get first-hand information about their lifestyles and important events happening in their countries. We even have discussions or debates from time to time. As a member of the global village, don't you agree that we should open our eyes to the world instead of restricting ourselves to this island? The Internet offers a cheaper way to do this. Before I have enough money and time to really visit other countries, the Internet will always be my tour guide and a great channel to communicate with exotic cultures and foreign friends.

6.2 常見的結論句寫法

常見的結論句寫法有用不同的文字重述主題句、總結前文下結論或評語、預測未來、提出呼籲等。除非還有下文，否則不可以在結論句中提及前文未提到的新內容。

1. 用不同的文字重述主題句(Restating the Main Idea)

If I Were Granted a Wish, What Would That Be?

I wish I could be the first ever to successfully develop a vehicle that is quick, comfortable, and most of all, driven by reusable energy! This is a time when oil crisis and fuel shortage leap onto the stage. At home, my parents often complain about the soaring price of fuel. And that complaint is commonly heard among adults. That makes me worried about the limited resources on our planet. A vehicle which can run solely on reusable energy, like solar power, or hydropower cell, will solve the problem. It can finally give us a chance to greatly refresh our earth, making a stride toward the goal on which we have worked so hard, that is, environmental conservation. <u>If I could be the first to invent such an environmentally friendly vehicle, it would greatly benefit the whole world.</u>

說明：結論句用不同文字重述主題句中的 ...I could be the first ever to successfully develop a vehicle...，再次強調文章的中心思想。

2. 總結前文下結論或評語(Making a Summary or Comment)

An Unforgettable Family Activity

My family and I travel often. However, one trip will have a place in my heart for all my life. Although my family traveled a lot, my grandmother, being old and unable to walk well, usually stayed at home alone instead of appreciating the world with us. So this summer, my father planned a trip especially for her. We went to her favorite place, Wuling. We marveled at the breathtaking scenery, heard the birds chirping and watched the spectacular waterfall. We also enjoyed a serene night together, chatting happily and watching the twinkling stars.

It felt so good to escape from the hustle and bustle of the city and be so close to my family. Nowadays, I get so busy that I hardly talk or do things with my family members, my grandmother in particular. The fantastic trip to Wuling gave me a chance to feel so connected with them. <u>It is definitely the most unforgettable activity I have done with my beloved family!</u>

說明：作者以自己的意見總結前文，以這次旅遊的重要意義作為結論。

3. 預測未來(Predicting)

If I Could Invent a New Product

If I could invent a new product, I would like to produce a machine which could detect a coming earthquake. The machine would boast the most accurate and sensitive sensor. As soon as it found an earthquake coming, it would send a warning message to every country via a satellite. The use of the satellite instead of any other device running on electricity was to make sure the machine could still work in a blackout.

The reason why I want to invent this product is that Taiwan is frequently plagued by earthquakes, many of which do a lot of harm to lives and properties of Taiwan's residents. If a machine like this could really come into existence, many tragedies caused by earthquakes would be avoided.

說明：作者預測若能發明地震預測儀器，未來將可避免許多災害。

4. 提出呼籲(Calling for Action)

What Can I Do to Stop Global Warming?

You can no longer tolerate the sweltering summer anymore, can you? Apparently, the temperature around the world has been soaring in the last decades. We have also noticed the startling news that the ice caps in polar areas are melting and causing the rise of the sea level. Therefore, a critical issue has emerged—what can we do to stop global warming?

First, the prime factor that contributes to global warming is the tremendous amount of fumes that we release into the air. As a result, we should drive less to efficiently reduce the emission of fumes. Taking public transportation or riding a bike is a good alternative. Secondly, we should avoid using air conditioners. Though the hot weather is intolerable, we have to understand that we're just making the environment even hotter. Finally, we should spread out the information and persuade people around us to follow these acts so as to gather the power of the public.

Since we all rely on Mother Earth for life, everyone should take the responsibility to protect her. And to stop global warming, no one can be exempt from the responsibility. Only with the efforts of each and every human being can we save our crying Mother Earth.

說明：結論句中作者就段落的內容向讀者提出呼籲：保護環境是每個地球子民的責任，請在看完文章後立即付諸行動！

ACTIVITY 2 請根據主題句以及支持句，從下面的句子中勾選出適合的結論句。

1

Internet and My Life

主題句：I didn't have very positive experiences with the Internet.

支持句：In the beginning, I had great fun exploring the new technology. I especially enjoyed sharing information through social networks such as Facebook or Instagram. Every day when I got free time, I used my smartphone to surf the Internet. I spent hours checking friends' newsfeeds. Gradually, I found myself so used to interacting with others through the Internet that I forgot the necessity of real-life communication. I barely talked to my parents and classmates. I became just like a net nerd. It seemed much easier for me to let out my secrets to my online friends through typing instead of uttering them to someone in person. I started to pay less attention to my studies and even gave up my all-time hobby— playing the piano. My parents and teachers were really concerned about my addiction to the Internet. Meanwhile, I also felt myself changing. Though I had many net friends, I felt lonely and isolated because I didn't get to hear the voices of my friends or family. I could only hear the prompt tones my cellphone made. At last, I decided to quit the habit and move on. _____

結論句：

_____ a. *I think we should all be thankful for people who invented the Internet. Among all the communications, the Internet is the cheapest and the most convenient one.*

_____ b. *From this experience, I think we do need much self-control when using the Internet to avoid some drawbacks brought by the useful tool.*

_____ c. *Instead of digging into piles of books, people nowadays find that information is only a few clicks away.*

One Thing I Regret Most

主題句：I was once a mischievous child who took an interest in playing practical jokes on my peers. As a matter of fact, seeing others fall for my pranks simply pleased me.

支持句：One day, I captured an insect and secretly placed it in a girl's lunch bag and urged her to open the bag during the lunch break. As the insect I earlier put in flew out, the girl gave out a piercing scream. Next to her I stood, feeling proud of my work. But all of a sudden, there was a loud bang. The girl I had teased fainted and fell to the ground. Fear seized me. After trying in vain to wake the girl up, I took her to the school nurse immediately. It was after an hour that the girl eventually regained consciousness. As the girl burst into tears, I apologized and apologized for what had happened. It was really fortunate for me that the girl and her parents accepted my apology and forgave me. _____

結論句：

_____ *a. To turn over a new leaf, I have stopped my evil humor since that day. I have learned that while some jokes can be tolerated, some jokes can get me into big trouble.*

_____ *b. If I had reached out a helping hand, the tragedy might have been avoided. How I wish I had spent a couple minutes listening to my classmate!*

_____ *c. If I had taken my mom's advice, I wouldn't have ended in such a miserable situation!*

 **3 請為下面段落補上結論句。**

What Taiwan Needs Most Now

Taiwan, once known as Formosa, meaning a beautiful island on the western Pacific Ocean, has earned the notorious epithet of "the greedy island" these years. With the rapid economic development in the late 1970s, this lovely island turned out to be a grimy, polluted junkyard, and so did the society. Many people become so selfish that all they care about is themselves. The connection between one and another has been broken gradually. What politicians know is how to take advantage of people rather than make a positive contribution to the country, with scandals and corruption disclosed almost every day. Therefore, I think what Taiwan needs most is a heroic leader with great responsibility as well as wisdom.

The one must be vigorous and intelligent enough to reform our society by enlightening and educating people. Passionate and patient as the leader is, he or she also needs others' assistance. It takes leadership to organize all elites in different realms to work smoothly together. _____

_____

An Unforgettable Trip

The most unforgettable activity I have ever done with my parents was a tour to Yangmingshan about ten years ago. I was very excited because I rarely went out with my family. I skipped about, everything seeming so pleasant to me. But it was in the afternoon that everything changed. I wanted to pick a purple flower on a steep cliff without getting my parents' permission. All of a sudden, I slipped and fell, with only one hand grabbing the edge of the cliff. How lucky I was that a passer-by witnessed this and saved my life! Shortly my parents came and thanked the passer-by with great gratitude. Then they scolded me harshly.

_____

_____

🍴 **漢堡祕方** ••

1. 可用不同的文字重述主題句、總結前文下結論或評語、預測未來，或提出呼籲等方式寫結論句。

2. 除非還有下文，否則不可以在結論句中提及前文所未提到的新內容。

•••

Note ✏️

CHAPTER 7

Unity, Coherence, and Cohesiveness
統一性、連貫性及緊密連接

　　統一性、連貫性及緊密連接就像是漢堡中的美乃滋，雖然人們常忽視它的存在，但是缺少了美乃滋的潤滑效果，口感可就生澀不順口了。因為美乃滋將麵包、生菜番茄、起司、牛肉等不同材料，緊密結合在一起，漢堡才會令人一口接一口，愈吃愈順口。寫作文也一樣，要顧及到每個句子與主題的統一性、全篇文章邏輯組織的連貫性，並用適當的轉承詞使文句緊密連接，才能寫出好文章。

7.1 統一性(Unity)

　　統一性是指文章有一個主題重心，所有的論點都必須支持主題。一個段落要有統一性，只能有一個主題，段落中所有的句子都要闡明主題句，不能有一個句子離題。

ACTIVITY 1 請細讀以下的段落，找出偏離主題的句子，並且回答下面的問題。

　　1 It is a routine for me to go to school from Monday to Friday. 2 Nevertheless, the daily journey is not at all unexciting because my arriving at the school is exactly a battle with time. 3 I never know if I can be punctual every day. 4 On hearing both of my alarm clocks ring at 8:00, I get up immediately though I can hardly open my eyes. 5 I get myself ready in 5 minutes, rush out of my dorm, and dash to the school straightly. 6 Every second is precious. 7 My school is located in downtown Taipei, about 5 minutes away from my dorm. 8 My classmates are all boys, which has both advantages and disadvantages. 9 Although it is nice to have girls around, I still like the fun and vibrant atmosphere in my class.

> 從第幾句開始偏離主題？這些句子談的是什麼事？為何偏離主題了？

 ACTIVITY 2 以下有三個段落，每一段中都有一句不切合主題的句子，請找出並畫上底線。

1

Laughter Is the Best Medicine

We can't avoid confronting frustrations in our life, but laughter can help us conquer them. For example, after we diligently prepare for an exam, we are full of confidence in getting good scores. However, the test is too difficult to pass. Some feel frustrated and depressed, others are in an awful mood all day, and still others even start doubting themselves. They are beaten harshly and can't stand up again, and I am no exception. Receiving bad grades always upsets me. But after reflecting on my failure, I refresh myself by letting out laughter. Sometimes I try going jogging, too. Then I regain confidence, being capable of putting myself back to work again. Next time when we face problems, we should never forget to laugh, and this best medicine will help us overcome any obstacles.

2

An Unforgettable Piece of Advice

My mother has always told me what to do and what not to do. But, as an adolescent, I seldom listen to her words. As a result, a terrible misery happened to me. One day I went out jogging, and Mom told me that I should do some stretches before I started. As always, I turned a deaf ear to her. On arriving at the park, I started running immediately, without doing any warm-up activity. Instead of running slowly, I dashed on the track as if someone were chasing me. I am one of the best runners in my class. Without enough warm-up and correct method of jogging, I soon felt exhausted five minutes later. Suddenly, a sharp pain seized me and forced me to stop. I sprained my ankle! It hurt so much that I couldn't help crying out. My mom sent me to the hospital the moment I waddled home with tears. The doctor said that I had to be on crutches for a month. I felt so regretful that I couldn't eat anything that night. If I had taken my mom's advice, I wouldn't have ended in such a miserable situation. What a fool I was!

An Unforgettable Piece of Advice

I was once afraid of joining any kind of activity, for I had no confidence in myself and feared failure. I turned down any invitation or opportunity to participate in a class campaign, and gradually isolated myself from the class. One day, my homeroom teacher and I had a chat. During our conversation, the teacher said, "Shawn, why don't you just enjoy the process, and stop worrying about the outcome?"

With my teacher's advice, I started to walk out of the ivory tower I had lived in for so long. I have great classmates in the class, including my best friend Jason. I restored my confidence and joined my classmates to take part in various activities, including sports events, choir contests, etc. I put all my strength into the process. As to the result, I learned to hope for the best and be prepared for the worst. This piece of advice not only helped me gain a new perspective on life, but also enabled me to gain fantastic experiences.

 漢堡祕方 文章寫得再好，全篇離題一定得不到分數，一兩句離題也一定會扣分。要如何避免離題的錯誤呢？

1. 擬好大綱並依大綱發展文章。
2. 不要賣弄最近剛學過、背過但與主題無關的句子。

7.2 連貫性(Coherence)

連貫性是指文章中所有的句子都要以某種邏輯串聯起來，如此讀者才會覺得文章流暢自然，也才能合理引導出結論句。以下介紹三種最常使用的方式，同學們在擬定大綱時，就應該先決定文章要點的順序下筆，以寫出組織嚴謹的文章。

 1. 時間順序(Time Order)

在敘述事件或說明程序時使用。一般都是採用順敘法，也就是按照事件或動作的先後順序安排；另外也可以採用倒敘法以追溯過去，但是這個方式並不適合初學者。

 2. 空間順序(Spatial Order)

在描述人、物或地方時使用。空間順序有以下幾種：

a. 由近到遠或由遠到近　　　　c. 由上到下或由下到上

b. 由左到右或由右到左　　　　d. 由裡到外或由外到裡

 3. 重要性順序(The Order of Importance)

在提出原因、結果、理由或比較事物時使用。常有作者將最重要的點放在最後提出，以營造高潮迭起的效果。但同學也可將最重要的點安排在第一點，以吸引閱卷老師的注意，提高印象分數。

以下三篇文章，是以The City I Live in為題，分別以時間順序、空間順序及重要性順序組織出通順流暢的段落。

範例一(時間順序)

　　Prosperous as Taipei now is, it was neither rich nor densely populated in the 19th century. Originally, the political and economic center was in central and southern Taiwan. However, as loads of goods were imported and exported through Tamsui Harbor and Keelung Harbor—the two biggest harbors in northern Taiwan, Taipei continued to grow larger, richer, and more prosperous. By the time the governor Liu Minchuan made massive improvements such as building railroads in Taipei, the city had already become the leading city of Taiwan, both economically and politically.

　　Now, Taipei is one of the world's busiest cities. Citizens living in Taipei represent some of the most successful people in Taiwan, or relatively the wealthier ones. Tall buildings rise into the skyline like rainforests, stretching with energy and vibrancy. Among these, Taipei 101 is probably the most representative one, standing like a miniature of the metropolis Taipei.

And in the future, what will Taipei city turn into? What role will it play in the global village? I guess we'll have to wait for the future to reveal itself. But one thing is for sure, this energetic city with limitless potential will continue to blossom, and it will certainly be as fun as it has always been!

說明： 這個段落採用順敘法，簡述臺北自名不見經傳，經過劉銘傳時期，至現代繁華的發展過程，並預測未來仍會蓬勃發展。

範例二（空間順序）

My hometown, a big city, has the largest population among all the cities in Taiwan. Still can't get it? Maybe a few hints will help you find out.

One of its landmarks is the renowned C.K.S. Memorial Hall, which stands nearby my beloved CK Senior High. Standing in the midst of the hall, you can feel a sense of magnificence and be amazed at the gigantic and splendid structures. Another famed location is the awe-inspiring Taipei 101, one of the tallest skyscrapers in the world. The bamboo-like shape and eminent height make it distinguished from all other buildings. Finally, I'm going to introduce my favorite spot around the city, namely Zhongshan Girls High School, which is only five minutes away from my home by car. I especially love to appreciate those adorable students in white uniforms and blue jackets. I can never take my eyes off them. Well, you probably have figured out the correct answer. That's right, it is the metropolis of Taiwan—Taipei City. With so many fascinating traits, Taipei is undoubtedly a wonderful place to live in!

說明： 這一段的邏輯採用空間順序，先由城市的南區、東區至北區，介紹作者心目中臺北市最有代表性的地點。

範例三（重要性順序）

If Los Angeles is a city with no center, then Taipei certainly is a city with centers everywhere.

Being the capital of its country, Taipei is where all the important political events take place. One can see all sorts of parades targeting different issues on the streets every few weeks. Places with political implications such as the C.K.S.

Memorial Hall and the 228 Peace Memorial Park also stand in this city. Aside from being the political center, Taipei is also the financial center. Statistics show that up to 80 percent of the international trading companies have set their branch offices in the city and its suburbs, not to mention the local business headquarters. What's more, Taipei is a city with the aroma of culture in its air. With the National Palace Museum, the National Theater, and the National Concert Hall located in the city, one can easily enjoy a feast of the finest art and performance in the world.

So stop wasting time and come to Taipei to experience the great beauty and enjoy the cultural variety of it right now.

說明：這個段落將三個要點依照重要順序排列，依序提出臺北為臺灣的政治中心 (political center)、金融中心(financial center)及文化中心(cultural center)。至於哪個最重要，則是由作者主觀認定的。

 **3** 請閱讀以下三篇以An Ideal English Classroom為題的文章，並分辨它們是用哪一種邏輯順序寫成的。

It is difficult for students to memorize each sentence and detail in textbooks. But using appropriate equipment can yield twice the result with half the effort.

A CD player can play the readings for students, and it can also sharpen students' listening skills and correct their pronunciation. A blackboard written with vocabulary is another necessity. Since students cannot focus on textbooks all the time, the blackboard placed on the corner provides another opportunity for learning. Additionally, an overhead projector makes learning easy and meaningful. Take the lesson "I Have a Dream" for example. By using the projector, the teacher can illustrate Dr. Martin Luther King's speech with pictures and films to explain the historical background, like how he fought for human rights and freedom. Then, with these vivid images, we can easily memorize the vocabulary, complex grammar, and even the development of history.

In short, an ideal English classroom should be equipped with educational media such as CD players, blackboards, and overhead projectors.

Ans: _____

An ideal English classroom is composed of three factors: a good environment, patient teachers, and motivated students.

First, the classroom must be well-illuminated and comfortable. It can protect students' vision, and the cozy environment can make students focus on their textbooks without being distracted by scorching hot weather or noises. Second, patient teachers are indispensable. A class is made up of about forty students, many of whom don't always get straight As. Therefore, patient teachers should not only teach students who perform well, but also care about students who get poor grades. Then it can really be ideal for students at every level. Most importantly, the main factor of an ideal English classroom is a group of motivated students. Every student can show his or her own ability and learn from one another. When they feel confused about some problems, they will browse the Net, go to libraries, or even do experiments themselves for answers.

If a classroom consists of these three factors, it will definitely be ideal for everyone.

Ans: _____

An ideal English classroom should adapt itself to fulfill the needs of students of different age groups. In kindergarten, children are not used to the new language, so teachers should encourage them to speak loudly. By singing songs and playing games, students can build up their confidence. In elementary school, students start to learn the alphabets and spelling, so the classroom can be decorated with lots of posters with letters in alphabetical order. The posters can be seen on the bulletin board, windows, or floors. By doing so, students can memorize alphabets without efforts.

In high school, students will face a decisive examination after three years of education. As the proverb goes, "Practice makes perfect." Teachers should give students numerous assignments and hold quizzes weekly to make sure that they score high in the entrance exam. Finally, in college students start to put theories into practice and provide their own opinions. Therefore, the seats in the classroom should be divided into groups so that students can discuss together efficiently.

An ideal English classroom is not a fixed one. Instead, it should vary with different educational stages to be suitable for every student.

Ans: _____

7.3 緊密連接(Cohesiveness)

緊密連接是指一個句子與下一個句子之間要環環相扣、關係緊密並且邏輯清楚。達到緊密連接的方法有二，即善用轉承詞及重複關鍵字。

 1. 善用轉承詞

轉承詞是文章中重要的線索，讓讀者對作者的語氣轉變做好心理準備。妥善使用轉承詞，能使句子與句子之間或者段落與段落之間文思與語氣的轉換順暢。以下列舉出常用的轉承詞：

文章的起始

說到	when it comes to/speaking of/as far as...is concerned
一般而言	generally speaking/in general/at large/on average
不證自明／不言可喻	it goes without saying that/it is needless to say that/there is no denying that/needless to say

文章的結論

總而言之	in short/in brief/in conclusion/to sum up/as a whole/to make a long story short/to summarize/in summary/in a word/in sum

交代時間順序

之後	later on/afterwards
同時	meanwhile/in the meantime/at the same time/simultaneously
最近	recently/lately
目前	now/nowadays/at present/for the time being
最後	finally/in the end/eventually/at last/in the long run
過去／未來	in the past/in the future
自…時起	from then on/from now on
到目前為止	so far/up to now/until today/until now

列舉的順序

首先	to begin with/in the first place/first of all/in the beginning
次之	second/secondly/next/in the second place/then
最後	lastly/last but not least/finally
最重要	most importantly/most important of all/above all

表因果關係

因為	because/since/now that/due to/owing to/thanks to/because of/on account of
因此	thus/therefore/so/as a result/consequently/accordingly/for this reason/hence

比較相同點

同樣地／像…	similarly/also/in the same way/likewise/similar to/like/just as

 對照相異之處

比起	compared with/in comparison with
然而	however/nevertheless/yet/still/but
相反地／不同於…	instead/on the contrary/conversely/unlike/in contrast to/with
一方面…，另一方面…	on the one hand...on the other hand.../for one thing...for another...

補充說明

例如	for example/for instance/take...for example/take...for instance/such as/including
換句話說	in other words/to put it another way/that is (to say)/namely
此外／而且	besides/in addition/moreover/what's more/also/furthermore
更…的是	what's better/worse/more
事實上	in fact/as a matter of fact/in reality

表讓步

雖然／儘管／即使	although/though/even though/even if/in spite of/despite/regardless of/notwithstanding/despite the fact (that)/while/whereas

 **ACTIVITY** 4 以下有三個段落，請依上下文從選項中選擇適合的轉承詞，使語氣流暢。請視需要調整字首大小寫。

 as time went by   however   as a result   then   as soon as

John and His Puppy

John was a cute little boy whose heart was filled with kindness and sympathy.

Since he was the only child in his family, John often felt lonely and wished to have someone to play with. [1]_____, on his seventh birthday, his parents gave him a lovely puppy, hoping it would be John's loyal companion. John loved the puppy very much. He named it after himself, using "Johnny" as its name. John took it to the park and played with it happily every day. It seemed as if his life would have been incomplete without Johnny. [2]_____, Johnny got lost in the park one day. John went to the toilet for only a few minutes, and [3]_____ he came back only to find that Johnny had vanished! John couldn't help crying at the thought of Johnny being cold and starving in the park alone at night. He kept searching for it but in vain. Johnny just didn't show up. [4]_____, John's hope gradually faded away. He decided to go home with reluctance and sorrow. To his surprise, [5]_____ he got near his home, he heard something familiar. Johnny was standing in front of the door, wagging its tail happily at him. John cried out with joy and held it tight in his arms, promising he would never let it go again.

2
first   secondly   lastly   in brief   therefore

Ideal Parents

Parents are the first people that their children encounter; [1]_____, they have crucial influences on children. The following are three important qualities that I think ideal parents should be equipped with. [2]_____, ideal parents must love their children deeply. A child who grows up in an environment without love will definitely lack the ability to love others. [3]_____, parents with a sense of responsibility should make their children behave themselves, so that the children will be well-bred and courteous when they grow up. People always think that the parents of criminals or rude people don't carry out their responsibilities well. [4]_____ and the most importantly, ideal parents should have a liberal mind. They should give heed to what their children

are thinking about and try to listen to their opinions on things. If children have different viewpoints on things, they should try to communicate with them calmly. ⁵_____, parents who can love their children, educate their children, and respect their children will make ideal parents.

3

unfortunately　　as a consequence　　in a word

most important of all　　in the past century

What Taiwan Needs Most Now

¹_____, Taiwan has made miraculous economic progress that has highly boosted the quality of our life. ²_____, we have been developing our country at the expense of our environment, making huge damage such as air pollution and soil contamination to our beloved land. ³_____, environmental protection is what I think the most crucial thing for Taiwan.

　　The government should not only be engaged in making severe laws to forbid people from doing such things as capturing endangered animals but also address the importance of recycling to everyone. ⁴_____, it makes a world of difference whether the belief of environmental protection is planted in everyone's heart. Taiwan will become a clean and scenic island if there is no garbage on the road. Tourists will come often, which will also benefit our sightseeing industry. ⁵_____, what the Taiwanese should consider is not which candidate we should vote for, but the issue of protecting our environment, which really has a great impact on our future. Let's make Taiwan a wonderful land for ourselves and our descendants.

段落與段落之間的連接

　　近年英文作文考試經常是引導式寫作,在提示中直接要求同學文分兩段。兩個段落之間如果能加上一句總結上文、開啟下文的句子,也對文章的緊密連接很有幫助。請參考下頁的範文:

The Advantages and Disadvantages of Genetic Engineering

Have you ever had potato chips or French fries? If you have, are you aware that the potatoes you ate may have been genetically changed? In the past, natural disasters used to cause damage to farmers' potatoes. Thanks to the development of genetic engineering, scientists can transfer a desired trait from one species to another. As a result, today's potatoes are not only frost-resistant but also more resistant to insects. They grow faster and require less fertilizer. <u>Isn't it wonderful that farmers now can have super potatoes that are easier to plant?</u>

<u>Unfortunately, the story is not so simple.</u> Human beings might face serious health risks after eating genetically modified foods because these foods also contain dangerous genes that are resistant to antibiotics. Recent research shows that the antibiotic resistant genes can be transferred from plants to bacteria, and make the bacteria so powerful that no antibiotic can kill them. In other words, human beings may die of certain diseases in the future because no medicine can kill the monster bacteria. Scientists should seriously brood over and monitor the long-term effects of genetic engineering so as not to jeopardize the health of human race.

說明：第一段結尾以提出問題Isn't it wonderful that farmers now can have super potatoes that are easier to plant? 來預告下一段的內容。第二段開頭 Unfortunately, the story is not so simple. 告知讀者第二段要呈現的內容沒有第一段那麼樂觀。這兩句話使兩個段落緊密地連接在一起。

ACTIVITY 5 請從A和B選項中，選出最適當的句子，以銜接下頁各篇文章中的兩個段落。

A. After hearing the encouraging and inspiring advice, I was consoled and I regained the strength to fulfill my goals.

B. It was a pleasant afternoon in summer.

1   One day, when I opened up an album, several photos fell out and broke the hourglass of time, which reminded me of a pleasant moment in life, an unforgettable moment with my friends.

_____ My friends and I went to Ba-li (八里) to ride bikes after the final exam. Arriving at Ba-li, we wasted no time in riding bikes together immediately. At that time, sky was like a clear square, a square wide enough for clouds to play a chasing game with us. Then a gentle breeze began to blow as we started to speed up. At that moment, riding bikes in the wind was like flying in the sky. With happy and carefree minds, we experienced senses of speed and excitement and enjoyed a pleasant moment in our life. In short, it is better to enjoy life with friends than to be alone. Though we are in different classes right now, we still keep in touch with each other, knowing that we had a pleasant moment together.

2   Shocked, upset and extremely disappointed. That's how I felt after being informed of the result of the entrance exam. Realizing the enormous gap between my dream and reality, I felt as if I had been pushed from the peak of the mountain of hope into the deep ocean of despair. I was almost unable to swim back to the shore. It was my father's advice, like a beacon light, that helped me find the way. He told me, knowing I was crazy about tennis, "Even Roger Federer, the man who dominates men's tennis, can't win every match. However, he would soon overcome the previous failure and get prepared for the next victory. This attitude is the reason why he is the champion and the one you should take right now."

_____ I knew from my heart if I kept myself locked in despair, there would be no way for me to succeed in the future. Therefore, I stood up again, against whatever would turn up in front of me.

2. 重複關鍵字

　　寫英文作文時，每句話都不能離開主題。同學可重複使用與主題相關的關鍵字，或是多用同義字、代名詞來指稱主題，將所有的句子緊緊扣住段落主旨。請閱讀以下的文章，並觀察畫底線的部分如何與主題緊密連接：

Do you have any idea about the highest building with bamboo-shaped structure in the world? Do you know which country holds the reputation of <u>the fruit kingdom</u>? The answer is <u>Taiwan</u>, a <u>subtropical island</u> like a <u>gem</u> shining on the ring of the Pacific Ocean. You must have heard of this <u>little island</u>, which caused the 17th century Portuguese to grant <u>it</u> the beautiful name, <u>Formosa</u>. In addition, small as this <u>island</u> is, <u>it</u> ranks high in the world economy. What's more, <u>Taiwan</u> gains astonishing achievements in the keen competitions in international baseball games. Since <u>Taiwan</u> is such a renowned country, you have to pay a visit to take a look at all the miracles <u>it</u> has made.

When visiting <u>Taiwan</u>, needless to say, you ought to appreciate one of the highest skyscrapers in the world—Taipei 101. The bamboo-shaped structure that penetrates into the clouds may take your breath away when you look up from below. Also, the large shopping mall offers you an access to the modern life of <u>Taiwan</u>, as well as <u>its</u> high economic development. To sum up, <u>Taiwan</u> is the most worth-traveling <u>tourist spot</u> you should never miss.

說明：此段中Taiwan出現了六次，並且用了其他的說法the fruit kingdom、subtropical island、gem、little island、Formosa、island、tourist spot和代名詞it來指稱Taiwan，讓讀者感覺每一句話都緊緊地圍繞在本文主題上，不僅避免有任何一句離題，也能達到緊密連接的效果。

ACTIVITY 6 請閱讀以下文章，將與主題相同的同義字或代名詞畫上底線。

An Ideal English Teacher

Learning English is never an easy job; however, a good English teacher can make the learning process more student-friendly and effective. Such a teacher should at least possess the following qualities. First of all, he or she must not focus only on the superficial meanings of words and articles. Instead, explaining the composition of words and the profound content of articles should come as the first priority. Second, this teacher would assign students to write reports on various topics in English and to have oral presentations on their works rather than simply giving testing papers targeting trivial grammar details. Last but definitely not the least, an ideal teacher must be equipped with an enthusiastic heart. Only with that can he or she make the beauty of this language alive beyond the lifeless textbooks. With the above-mentioned qualities, an ideal English teacher will become a reality.

ACTIVITY 7 同學使用代名詞時最容易犯的錯誤就是任意轉換人稱而沒有一致性。請細讀以下的例子，注意代名詞的使用是否正確。若不正確，請加以改正。

Students should plan their time carefully so that <u>you</u> can have enough time for <u>your</u> schoolwork. If <u>you</u> always spend a lot of time chatting with classmates, <u>you</u> can never finish <u>your</u> homework. <u>We</u> should know when to relax and when to work hard.

漢堡祕方 寫文章還要注意到：‧‧‧‧‧‧‧‧‧‧‧‧‧‧‧‧‧‧‧‧‧‧‧‧‧‧‧‧‧

1. 統一性——文章有一個主題重心，所有的論點都必須支持主題。不能有一個句子離題。

2. 連貫性——文章中所有的句子都要以某種邏輯(時間順序、空間順序、重要性順序等)串聯起來，如此文章才會流暢自然。

3. 緊密連接——善用轉承詞或代名詞及同義字，使得一個句子與下一個句子之間、一個段落與下一個段落之間要環環相扣、關係緊密並且邏輯清楚。

CHAPTER 8

Avoiding Common Errors
避免常見錯誤

　　相信大家在吃漢堡的時候，吃到蛋殼、菜蟲或骨頭，或是點了雞肉漢堡卻吃到魚肉，一定會覺得倒足了胃口。同樣地，閱卷老師在批改同學的英文作文時，也希望讀到自然流暢、文法錯誤少的作品。這一章整理出同學常犯的錯誤，希望同學能藉由練習，減少寫作時犯錯的機會。

8.1 注意正確地斷句(Avoiding Comma Splices and Run-On Sentences)

　　兩個獨立子句之間應該有正確的標點或用連接詞連接，如果沒有注意到，就會有不正確地斷句的問題產生。請參考以下例句：

錯　誤	正　確
1. Our school chorus won the first place in the national music contest it will give a performance at the concert hall tonight. →沒有用正確的標點及連接詞連接兩個子句。	Our school chorus won the first place in the national music contest, **and** it will give a performance at the concert hall tonight.
2. Zach has always been optimistic, however, he is deeply frustrated by this failure. →僅用逗點連接，沒有正確地使用標點。	Zach has always been optimistic. **However**, he is deeply frustrated by this failure. 或 Zach has always been optimistic; **however**, he is deeply frustrated by this failure.

EXERCISE 1 請判斷以下句子是否正確地斷句。若不正確，請訂正。

1. Most children are the happiest in kindergarten. Because there they have no tests or homework.

2. Raising children is not like raising pets. The former takes much more responsibility and patience.

3. Rose finally accepted my invitation to sing at my party I have begged her for two weeks.

4. It was unbearably hot, I decided to treat myself two scoops of ice cream.

5. The umpire was unfair, therefore, the spectators were annoyed.

6. I take piano class with Miss Leonard, she studied music at Juilliard School.

7. The assignment contains two parts a review exercise included.

8. Biking is healthy, moreover, it is environment-friendly.

9. Your idea is brilliant, it's practical too.

10. Because of the economic depression fewer and fewer college graduates choose to go abroad for further studies.

8.2 注意句子的完整(Avoiding Sentence Fragments)

　　一般來說每個句子(除了祈使句、感嘆句及一些慣用諺語之外)都會有一個主詞和一個動詞。另外，連接詞帶領的子句為從屬子句，還需要一個主要子句句意才會完整。句子完整了才能打上句點；如果忽略了，就可能產生語意不清的破碎句子。請參考以下例句：

不完整	完整
1. A 5,000-year-old tree standing on the hill. →只是一個片語，不能獨立成一句。	After an hour's hiking, you will see a 5,000-year-old tree standing on the hill.
2. Because eating at a cafeteria is the most economical. →由because帶領的子句只能作從屬子句，不能獨立成一句。	Because eating at a cafeteria is the most economical, I dine there every day.

EXERCISE 2 請閱讀以下的句子，判斷是否有不完整的句子。如果有，請改寫為正確的句子。

1. Writing a good composition is not difficult. As long as you read extensively and write constantly.

2. Even though it is hot in summer. The herbal doctor advises that you should not eat or drink anything ice-cold.

3. This year, the conference will be held in Kyoto, Japan.

4. Unable to concentrate in class because my classmates were noisy.

5. Mt. Jade, the highest mountain in Taiwan, is about 4,000 meters high.

6. Mr. Friedman, who runs a stray dog shelter. He believes that all animals have the right to live.

7. Although a strong typhoon was predicted. The climbers decided to go into the mountains.

8. Having popcorn and watching films at home on Saturday nights.

9. What a lovely kitten!

10. After new teachers work for about five years. They start to feel confident of themselves.

8.3 注意主詞、動詞在人稱及單複數的一致性 (Subject-Verb Agreement)

　　英文的動詞有人稱及單複數的變化，而其變化視主詞而定。在較長的句子中，不管主詞與動詞之間插入多少修飾語，還是要找到真正的主詞來判定動詞的人稱及單複數。請參考以下例句：

1. The number of the students present **is** 40.

（主詞number為一個數字，因此動詞為單數。）

A number of students **are** going to participate in the contest.

（主詞students為複數，因此動詞為複數。）

2. There **are** several deserted houses in the village.

（主詞為houses，因此動詞為複數。）

3. A piece of bread and butter **is** what I want for breakfast.

（主詞bread and butter視為一樣食物，為單數，因此動詞為單數。另外如a cup and saucer或spaghetti and meatballs也是如此。）

4. Economics **is** a difficult subject.

(主詞economics經濟學為單數，因此動詞為單數。常見以s結尾卻是單數的名詞還有measles、news、genetics、physics、mathematics、politics等。)

5. Jason is one of the students who **are** overachievers.

(關係子句中的主詞為關係代名詞who，而who的先行詞為students為複數，因此動詞為複數。)

6. The family **is/are** taking a vacation in Hawaii.

(主詞family單複數同形，因此動詞單複數皆可；不過單數時指的是一個團體，而複數時則是指其中的成員。這一類的名詞還有class、team、committee、staff、jury、audience等。)

7. The media **were** believed to have great influence on people's opinions.

(主詞media為medium的複數，因此動詞為複數。常見的例子還有bacteria為bacterium的複數；data為datum的複數；phenomena為phenomenon的複數；crises為crisis的複數；analyses為analysis的複數。)

8. Either you or I **am** responsible for the accident.

Neither the teacher nor the students **are** having a good time at the assembly.

連接詞			動詞單複數
	A or	B	
Either	A or	B	
Neither	A nor	B	動詞的單複數與B一致
Not only	A but also	B	
A	as well as	B	
A	together with	B	
A	along with	B	動詞的單複數與A一致
A	with	B	

9. Everyone who heard the story **sympathizes** with the little boy.

Almost every classroom in the school **is** equipped with Internet access.

Most of the children **are** running around in the playground.

Few **are** chatting in the classroom.

主　詞	動　詞
each、every、either、neither等代名詞或形容詞	單數
不定代名詞如someone、somebody、anyone、anybody、everyone、everybody、nobody、another、no one、one、little、any、much、none、the other	單數
不定代名詞如few、both、many、several、others	複數
不定代名詞如all/some/most + of + the可數名詞	複數
不定代名詞如all/some/most + of + the不可數名詞	單數

10. Five years **is** a long time.

Ten divided by five **equals** two.

Ten meters **is** a short distance.

Six hundred dollars **is** not a small sum.

(主詞five years視為一段時間，ten視為一個數字，ten meters視為一個長度，six hundred dollars視為一筆錢，因此動詞為單數。)

EXERCISE 3　　請圈選正確的動詞。

1. A list of items you want to buy (is/are) a good reminder when doing grocery shopping.

2. Each of the dresses in our store (is/are) uniquely designed.

3. Neither of Frank's parents (is/are) fond of his girlfriend.

4. There (is/are) a computer with Internet access in each of the classrooms.

5. Not only my parents but also I (am/are) anxious about the result.

6. The data on the Internet (is/are) not necessarily true.

7. Nine months (is/are) how long it takes for a pregnancy to go to full term.

8. The number of runners in yesterday's marathon (was/were) over 3,000.

9. Green tea as well as grape seeds (is/are) believed to be rich in antioxidants.

10. Spaghetti and meatballs (is/are) my favorite Italian dish.

8.4 正確使用代名詞(Agreement of Pronouns and Antecedents)

代名詞的單複數、人稱、格及性別都應該要與先行詞一致。請參考例句：

1. No one in the world swims as fast as he. (as為連接詞，後面接主格。)

2. My sister wins more attention than I (do). (than為連接詞，後面接主格。)

3. It was I who foresaw the outcome. (be動詞後面接補語，不用受格。)

4. Give the money to whoever needs it. (關係代名詞whoever是關係子句的主詞，應用主格。)

5. Who do you think will be elected president? (do you think為插入語，省略不看；who是will be的主詞，應用主格。)

6. Whom do you think we should invite? (do you think為插入語，省略不看；whom是invite的受詞，應用受格。)

7. The college offered Sally and me admission. (me作offer的受詞，應用受格。)

另外，應避免代名詞指涉不清楚的狀況。請參考例句：

不清楚	清　楚
1. This latest model of cellphone has a power-saving battery, which I think everyone should buy. →which指的到底是cellphone還是battery？	This latest model of cellphone, which I think everyone should buy, has a power-saving battery.
2. His bag indicated that he came from a great high school, and I think that he missed it. →it指的到底是bag還是school？	His bag indicated that he came from a great high school, and I think that he missed his old school.
3. Angelica told her sister that she needed to move on after the divorce. →she指的到底是Angelica還是her sister？	Angelica told her sister to move on after the divorce. 或 Angelica said, "Sister, you need to move on after the divorce."

EXERCISE 4　請圈選正確的代名詞。

1. The Beatles created many popular songs; (its/their) music is still enjoyed all over the world today.

2. There is little similarity between my sister and (I/me).

3. Students were told to read the analyses and critique (its/their) arguments.

4. Do you mind (me/my) coming along?

5. The lady to (who/whom) I was introduced was really charming.

6. After three months' campaign, everybody is ready to cast (their/his or her) vote.

7. I don't know anybody who is as rich as (he/him).

8. Do you know (who/whom) sent this package?

9. Peter is the contestant (who/whom) we think we will give the award to.

10. Peter is the contestant (who/whom) we think will win the award.

請修改以下的句子，使代名詞的指涉清楚。

11. My Gucci dress was not in the closet, which I promised to lend my roommate.

_____

12. Carl told Nick that everyone in class was keeping their fingers crossed for him.

_____

8.5 正確使用修飾語(Avoiding Dangling and Misplaced Modifiers)

　　修飾語(分詞、不定詞、形容詞、副詞等)常被用來修飾句中的名詞或動詞，但是如果不小心，可能會造成語意模稜兩可或不合邏輯。請參考以下例句：

不正確	正確
1. Dozing off in class, the ringing of the bell surprised him. →打瞌睡的應該是he而不是the ringing of the bell。	Dozing off in class, he was surprised by the ringing of the bell.

2. On entering the room, Mom was surfing the Internet.
→Mom不可能同時entering the room並surfing the Internet。

On entering the room, I found Mom surfing the Internet.

3. To efficiently cope with stress, nutritious food must be eaten.
→food不會有to cope with stress的需要。

To efficiently cope with stress, one must eat nutritious food.

4. When only five years old, my mother took me to Disneyland.
→不可能有五歲的媽媽。

When I was only five years old, my mother took me to Disneyland.

5. A famous painting was displayed in the museum that was painted by Jean-François Millet.
→that引導的形容詞子句離修飾對象太遠。

A famous painting that was painted by Jean-François Millet was displayed in the museum.

6. The student took the exam carefully looking for any possible mistakes.
→carefully修飾的動詞不知道是took還是looking。

The student took the exam carefully, looking for any possible mistakes.
或
The student took the exam, looking carefully for any possible mistakes.

7. During the hunger strike, the protester nearly ate nothing for 200 hours.
→nearly修飾的對象應該是200 hours而不是ate。

During the hunger strike, the protester ate nothing for nearly 200 hours.

EXERCISE 5 請判斷以下句子中的修飾語是否正確。若不正確，請訂正。

1. Seeing her child off at the airport, tears welled up in the mom's eyes.

→ _____

2. If lost, you cannot replace the ticket.

→ _____

3. When taking the school bus, it suddenly occurred to me that I forgot to bring my report which was due today.

→ _____

4. To make a good bowl of beef noodles, many ingredients are needed to prepare the broth.

→ _____

5. Broadcast at 6:30 a.m., Ian usually has time for the radio program before school.

→ _____

6. The two backpackers decided to end their tour early carrying heavy luggage.

→ _____

7. My grandfather has spent 50 years doing research on the teaching of Confucius, who is 70 years old now.

→ _____

8. We expect to visit the town where Shakespeare was born in summer vacation.

→ _____

9. The students complained that they barely have enough time to complete the assignments.

→ _____

10. It was nice of Jackie to bring the sick bird to the vet that he found in the woods.

→ _____

8.6 注意平行結構要確實對等(Parallelism)

　　使用對等連接詞連接的句子其實不難，但是同學常常忽略對等連接詞所連接的每個部分，在詞性上、結構上必須對等。

不對等	對　等
1. Whoever elected as the president should be <u>responsible</u>, <u>farseeing</u>, and <u>have charisma</u>. →and所連接的結構不對等。	Whoever elected as the president should be responsible, farseeing, and <u>charismatic</u>.
2. Besides English, I plan either <u>to learn French</u> or <u>Spanish</u> in college. →either...or...所連接的結構不對等。	Besides English, I plan to learn either <u>French</u> or <u>Spanish</u> in college.
3. Frankie's English <u>vocabulary</u> is larger than <u>any other student</u> in the class. →比較的結構不對等。	Frankie's English vocabulary is larger than any other <u>student's</u> in the class.

EXERCISE 6 請判斷以下句子中的平行結構是否正確。若不正確，請訂正。

1. In my opinion, the flavor of Tiramisu is better than Brownie.

2. Situated on the hill were a chapel, water fountain, and a line of palm trees.

3. Those young people stood in line, bought their tickets, and then they ran directly to the roller coaster.

4. The change in the educational system not only affected the students but also the teachers.

5. No one's passion about science is equal to Eliza.

6. The children always have and always will remember their father's dying words.

7. Harry was cold, tired, and wishes to have something to eat.

8. It is obvious that my parents love me more than Monica.

9. I neither know where he is going nor when he is leaving.

10. Living in Tokyo is as expensive, if not more expensive than, living in New York.

8.7 正確使用標點符號(Punctuation)

在標點符號中，同學最不容易掌握的是破折號、刪節號、分號、冒號及引號前後的標點。

 I. 破折號(Dash —)

例 句	功 能
1. Mr. Harper's children—Tim, Rose, and Frank—held a grand birthday party for him.	引導同位語
2. At the age of three—such was his musical genius—Mozart was able to play the piano.	加強語氣
3. Bruce told me—can you believe it?—that he had got married 7 times before.	語氣轉變
4. "I know it's a great chance. But—but, I have very serious stage fright."	遲疑的語氣

II. 刪節號(Ellipsis ...)

例　句	功　能
"Build me a son, O Lord, ...strong enough to know when he is weak, and brave enough to face himself when he is afraid...."	三個句點表示省略引述，如在結尾則需第四個句點來表示句子結束。

 III. 分號(Semicolon ;)

例　句	功　能
1. Sophie's father loves her very much. However, he isn't able to spend much time with her. 或 Sophie's father loves her very much; however, he isn't able to spend much time with her.	兩個子句中間如果沒有連接詞連接，有兩種方式可使得標點正確。第一種是打上句點，分成兩個完整句子；第二種是打上分號，分號後面的子句開頭要小寫。
2. Stephen Spielberg's works are entertaining; they are full of imagination.	分號可連接兩個子句。
3. The magician is going to perform in Taipei, Taiwan; Tokyo, Japan; Seoul, Korea; and Kuala Lumpur, Malaysia.	含有對等連接詞的子句中，如果已使用許多逗點，可使用分號來使句子清楚。

IV. 冒號(Colon :)

例　句	功　能
1. There is only one way for you to win the contest: good teamwork.	詳細解釋前面的敘述。
2. Dear Sir: ...	正式信件開頭的問候語。現代信件較不正式者也可用逗點。
3. The most expensive cities to live in are the following metropolises: New York, Tokyo, and London.	用於列舉。注意需有先行詞，冒號前面的子句必須完整。

V. 引號(Quotation Marks " ")

例 句	功 能
1. We read "Romeo and Juliet" in the drama class.	用於小型的或短的歌曲、電視節目、詩、文章、劇本的標題等。
2. ・Mom said, "It's time that you stood on your own feet." ・"I am afraid," the doctor said, "that the patient won't make it."	用於直接引句,若有逗點或句點要放在引號裡面。
3. A hundred times I said, "I am sorry"; yet he wouldn't forgive me.	用於直接引句,若有冒號或分號要放在引號外面。
4. ・The foreign visitor asked, "May I beg your pardon?" ・Did the professor said, "The paper is due in two weeks"?	用於直接引句,問號或驚嘆號的位置要看整個問句或感嘆句而定。
5. In America, a "homely" or "plain"-looking person is in fact ugly.	用來暗示字詞的特殊意思或絃外之音。

EXERCISE 7 請為以下的句子填入適當的標點符號。

1. Couldn't you say _____ Excuse me _____ _____

2. I think you shouldn't come clean about the mistake _____ oh, have you confessed the whole thing?

3. Last weekend I read O. Henry's _____ The Last Leaf _____ and I was deeply touched.

4. "Stay alert _____ _____ reminded the tour guide _____ _____ to the pickpockets when you travel in Italy."

5. Our teachers _____ Mr. Green, Mrs. Kelly, and Miss. Kennedy _____ will join us in the fund-raising garden party.

6. Your compositions are graded according to the following _____ content, organization, diction, grammar, and mechanics.

7. Dear Madam _____ I wish I had checked my email box earlier. I wonder if I could still sign up for the summer camp.

8. The best gift for your mother is inexpensive _____ tell her you love her.

9. That cute and sweet guy is _____ you have probably guessed _____ already married to somebody else.

10. "Watch out _____ _____ cried Jasmine. _____ There is a car coming _____ _____

8.8 正確使用There is/are.... 的句型

　　There is/are.... 的句型同學在國中階段就學過了，同學寫作文時也很喜歡使用這個基礎句型，但是卻很少使用正確。要注意這個句型是用來表示某物存在於某地的狀態，後面只能接片語或分詞作為修飾語，不能再加普通動詞。如果該句子裡的動詞很重要，則建議不要使用此句型。

不正確	正　確
1. There are some scientists <u>work</u> hard to cure AIDS. →scientists後面應該要接修飾語，不可以接普通動詞work。	There are some scientists <u>working</u> hard to cure AIDS. →將work改為分詞working。或 Some scientists are <u>working</u> hard to cure AIDS. →不使用There are句型。
2. There was a man <u>dozed</u> off under the tree. →man後面只能接man的修飾語，不可以接普通動詞dozed。	There was a man <u>dozing</u> off under the tree. →將dozed改為分詞dozing。或 A man was <u>dozing</u> off under the tree. →不使用There was句型。

EXERCISE 8　　請使用There is/are.... 的句型，將下列句子翻譯成英文。

1. 門口有一隻流浪貓在喵喵叫。

_____

2. 委員會裡有八位男性和五位女性。

_____

請使用There is/are.... 以外的句型，將下列句子翻譯成英文。

3. 那年有五個颱風侵襲臺灣。

_____

4. 這學期有兩位學生輟學。

_____

8.9 注意用字的正確性(Diction and Spelling)

有些字詞，因為用法相近或是拼法相似，常常會被誤用。在此列出同學最常犯的錯誤，請同學藉由說明及練習避免不必要的錯誤。

I. 分辨cost/take/spend

cost/cost/cost *vt.* 花費(金錢)；付出代價；使犧牲掉(主詞是物或it，作花費講時只有主動)

take/took/taken *vt.* 花費(時間)；需要某些條件(主詞是物或it，作花費講時只有主動)

spend/spent/spent *vt.* 花費(時間、金錢)；度過(主事者是人，作花費講時可用主動或被動)

EXERCISE 9

1. The digital camera _____ me twelve thousand dollars.
2. Crossing the mountains _____ the expedition group about ten days.
3. His obsession with gambling _____ him his job.
4. Most of her time was _____ on her business.
5. Jessica _____ about three hours having her hair done.
6. It _____ him just one hour to compose the piece of music.
7. It _____ Sophia about one million dollars to renovate her old house.
8. It _____ efforts and strong will to follow your dream.
9. Ben _____ the weekend with his friends at the beach.

II. 分辨rise/raise/arise

rise/rose/risen *vi.* 起床；上升；起身；升遷；升起

raise/raised/raised *vt.* 舉起；提高；養育；募款

arise/arose/arisen *vi.* 發生

EXERCISE 10

1. I usually _____ at six o'clock every morning.

2. The divorce rate has _____ steadily since 1950.

3. _____ your hand if you have any questions.

4. Many universities plan to _____ their tuition.

5. More nuclear power problems will _____ if we do nothing about it.

6. After class students picked up their bags and _____ to leave.

7. The soldier _____ to the rank of major.

8. They are _____ money for the homeless.

9. Both the sun and the moon _____ in the east.

10. I was born and _____ in southern Taiwan.

III. 分辨sometime/sometimes/some time/some times

sometime *adv.* 某時

sometimes *adv.* 有時候，偶爾

some time 一些時間

some times 幾次

EXERCISE 11

1. I think I met that woman _____ before.

2. I want to spend _____ hanging out with my friends.

3. I have been to Paris _____.

4. _____ I doze off in class.

IV. 分辨lie/lie/lay

lie/lied/lied/lying *vi.* 說謊；欺騙

lie/lay/lain/lying *vi.* 躺臥；(東西)平放；位於

lay/laid/laid/laying *vt.*; *vi.* 放置；產卵

EXERCISE 12

1. It's bad for the eyes to _____ in bed and read.

2. This hen _____ seven eggs a week.

3. Kathy _____ her cup down and went to answer the door.

4. Jeff _____ about his height in order to become a flight attendant.

5. Taiwan _____ to the east of China.

6. Tina _____ when she said she was too sick to come.

V. 分辨little/few

little *adj.* 少的(修飾不可數名詞，比較級為less，最高級為least)

few *adj.* 少的(修飾可數名詞，比較級為fewer，最高級為fewest)

EXERCISE 13

1. The mayor is proud that in the city _____ citizens are addicted to alcohol or drugs.

2. Snow is much _____ common in Taiwan than in Japan.

3. Of all the language courses offered in this institute, Latin has the _____ students.

4. I have very _____ knowledge about what life was like in Iran.

5. This town attracted _____ tourists than last year after the outbreak of the disease.

6. Due to our limited budget, we chose to stay at the _____ expensive hotel when we traveled.

VI. 分辨everyday/every day

everyday 是形容詞，相當於daily

every day 是頻率副詞，修飾動詞

EXERCISE 14

1. _____ my father works in a company from 8 a.m. to 5 p.m., and then he drives a cab for five hours till midnight.

2. Surfing the Internet has become part of my _____ life.

VII. 分辨used to V/be used to V-ing/be used to V

S + used to + V　曾經、過去常常做某事，而現在已經不做了

S + be/get used to + N/V-ing　習慣於某事

S + be used to + V　某物被用來做某事

EXERCISE 15

1. After living in Taiwan for 20 years, Ronald _____ eating Chinese food and drinking tea.

2. The sunscreen _____ protect your skin from being sunburned.

3. We _____ swim and fish in that river, but it's too dirty now.

VIII. 分辨hard/hardly

hard *adj.* 硬的；困難的

　　　adv. 努力地；猛烈地

hardly *adv.* 幾乎不；簡直不

EXERCISE 16

1. Samuel tried very _____ to get on the school team, but he failed.

2. I was so exhausted that I could _____ open my eyes.

3. Multiplication and division are too _____ for a three-year-old child.

IX. 分辨maybe/may be

maybe *adv.* 大概，可能，或許(等於perhaps)

may be　助動詞 + be動詞(後面接形容詞或名詞作補語)

EXERCISE 17

1. You _____ right. The plane might have been delayed because of the storm.

2. _____ you should tell your teacher what really happened.

X. 形容詞與副詞的使用時機

1. 修飾動詞的時候，使用副詞。但是在感官動詞(如：look、smell、taste、feel、sound)及連綴動詞(如：be、become、seem、appear、remain、stay、grow、feel)之後接的詞修飾主詞，要用形容詞。請參考例句：

   · When you talk to somebody, you should look <u>directly</u> into the other person's eyes. (directly修飾的是動詞，所以用副詞)

   · The old lady looked <u>happy</u> holding her grandson in her hands. (happy修飾的是主詞，所以用形容詞)

2. 在名詞字尾加上ly，會使詞性變成形容詞，而不是副詞。

   · Everything was nice about the hotel, only that the receptionist wasn't <u>friendly</u>.

3. 有些字的形容詞及副詞完全不同形，但意義相同；而有些字可同時當作形容詞及副詞，但所代表的字義不同。

   good *adj.* 好的

   well *adv.* 好地

   　　adj. 健康的

EXERCISE 18 　　請分辨下列句子中的形容詞或副詞使用是否正確。如果不正確，請訂正。

1. The taste of the cake is as smooth as that of the ice cream.

2. I felt badly about not being able to help the vagabond in ragged clothes.

3. The donuts smelled sweetly when I passed by the pastry shop.

4. Jonathan looked really happily. Serena must have accepted his proposal.

5. Doctors should explain to their patients their conditions in homely terms.

6. I feel confidently that I will pass all subjects with flying colors this semester.

7. The boy felt good after his broken bones healed.

8. I always feel well having a bowl of shaved ice on a boiling hot summer day.

9. The car was going too fastly to stop when the light turned red.

10. When we were speaking ill of our boss, he appeared sudden.

XI. 分辨as/like

as和like都有「像，如」的意思，但是在這個意思之下，as是連接詞，後面接子句；like是介系詞，後面接名詞。

EXERCISE 19

1. After you swim for five minutes, the water won't be as cold _____ you imagine.

2. Phelps swims _____ a fish. No wonder he won eight gold medals in the Beijing Olympic Games.

3. My son's girlfriend is _____ a daughter to me.

4. Do in Rome _____ Romans do.

Note ✏️

CHAPTER 9

Writing Samples and Exercises

寫作範例及練習

　　依據大考中心公布的考試說明，英文作文考試在主題上多與考生日常生活與學習範疇密切配合。而在題目中設定情境，並指定寫作任務，例如寫信、描述圖片或評論特定主題等，讓考生透過觀察或反思等方式，發表自己的想法或意見，從而達到以英文解決任務的目標，即是所謂的「任務型寫作」。其主要測驗的文體及形式如下：

形　式	文　體
簡函寫作	敘述文(narration)、描寫文(description)、說明文(exposition) 其中，說明文的文類大致上包含：
看圖寫作	1. 舉例法(illustration/providing examples) 　　2. 提出理由法(giving reasons)
圖表寫作	3. 定義法(definition) 　　4. 因果關係法(cause and effect) 　　5. 過程分析法(process analysis)
主題寫作	6. 比較對照法(comparison and contrast)

　　為了讓同學能清楚掌握大學入學考試各種文體與形式，以下便依序提供簡函寫作、看圖寫作與圖表寫作、敘述文、描寫文、及六種說明文的寫作範例及練習題目，同學並可利用本章最後所附的「寫作練習卷」實際練習寫作，並用其後隨附的「寫作評估表」評估寫作成果。

✎ 漢堡祕方 ••

　　雖然大考英文作文的字數要求通常是約120字，但是120字的文章其實很短，內容不可能很豐富。若要得到高分，同學可將文章加長到150−180字。但也不需刻意超過200字，以免適得其反給閱卷老師負面印象。

I. 簡函寫作

1. 信件的開頭應該為問候語Dear XX: ...，冒號也可以用逗號代換。

2. 信件的結尾應該用Sincerely yours、Sincerely、Yours等結尾語，然後在次行署名。

3. 如果要加日期，則加在全信的右上角。

〈參考範文〉

提示： 你最好的朋友最近迷上電玩，因此常常熬夜，疏忽課業，並受到父母的責罵。你(英文名字必須假設為 Jack 或 Jill)打算寫一封信給他／她(英文名字必須假設為 Ken 或 Barbie)，適當地給予勸告。

請注意： 必須使用上述的 Jack 或 Jill 在信末署名，不得使用自己的真實中文或英文名字。(101 年學測)

Dear Ken,

　　We haven't played basketball together for quite a while. After school, you always rush home right away. As far as I know, you are addicted to video games and stay up almost every day. What's more, your grades have dropped dramatically. I heard that your parents get mad and scold you all the time. I'm concerned about you and hope that you are doing well.

　　It can't be denied that playing video games is exciting. Yet, in spite of this, I'd like to advise that you regard it as nothing but a way to help you relax and relieve your tension occasionally. However, don't forget playing basketball can do the same! Do you remember the good times we used to have on the basketball court? Why don't you cut down on playing the games and come back to the court? I'm looking forward to playing basketball with you soon!

Yours,

Jack

說明： 作者寫信勸告好友時，第一段先以很久沒一起打籃球了對好友動之以情並對好友表達關心，第二段則是以期待能再一起打籃球來委婉勸說好友減少打電玩的時間。

〈**Topics for Exercise**〉

1. 請寫一封信給你想申請的校系。第一段說明該校系吸引你的原因,第二段推薦自己的優點,說服對方錄取你。

2. 請寫一封信給你的校長。第一段抱怨學校的某種措施不合理,第二段具體說明學校應該如何改進。

II. 看圖寫作與圖表寫作

1. 有圖片或圖表的作文題目為近幾年大考常見題型,種類可大致分為連環圖或單張圖的描述、兩張圖的擇一論述,以及圖表的判讀論述。有時這些圖片或圖表亦可作為主題寫作的基礎,本書將這類相關寫作題目皆統整在這邊一併解說。

2. 連環圖或單張圖的描述:

   (1) 一定要看懂每張圖的情節,寫作時每張圖都要交代到。

   (2) 可以有主題句;也可以先點出時間、地點,接著詳細敘述圖片內容,最後下一個簡單的結論。

   (3) 為避免代名詞太多造成混淆,建議可為圖中每個角色取名字;也可以用第一人稱,將自己當作主角。

   (4) 整篇的時態以簡單過去式較適宜。

3. 兩張圖的擇一論述:

   建議選擇自己比較有把握說明的那一張圖片來作論述,例如可先依據自己的字彙量斟酌考慮後,才決定寫作的內容。

4. 圖表的判讀論述:

   先看清楚圖表所傳達的資訊,注意圖表中值得探討的重點,並根據題目指示加以分析論述。

◉ 〈參考範文 1〉

提示：請仔細觀察以下三幅連環圖片的內容，並想像第四幅圖片可能的發展，
　　　寫一篇涵蓋所有連環圖片內容且有完整結局的故事。(103 年學測)

　　Yesterday, my brother and I left school together for home. As usual, we were using smartphones while walking on the road. We were so absorbed in using our phones that none of us noticed what lay in front of us. Just when I was looking at my phone, I bumped into a tree. Feeling dizzy right away, I dropped the phone on the ground. Right behind me was a mother with her child. The mother was shocked to see what happened to me.

　　Meanwhile, my brother listened to his music with high volume, and he didn't realize that he was walking in the middle of the road. Thus, when a car approached from behind, he was not aware of it at all. The driver was so mad that he honked the horn repeatedly. Finally, one of the passers-by rushed to pat my brother on the shoulder and told him about a car behind him. My brother moved to the side of the road immediately. He took off his headphones and finally heard me crying over my bleeding forehead and the broken phone.

說明：作者用字遣詞適宜且生動，並且善用表時間順序的轉承詞，以圖中連貫的主
　　　題「走路時用手機」為主要的發展架構，清楚描述每一張圖片的內容，第四
　　　幅圖片的內容則發揮創意，使故事有合理的結局。

〈參考範文 2〉

提示：請觀察以下有關某家賣場週年慶的新聞報導圖片，並根據圖片內容想像
其中發生的一個事件或故事，寫一篇英文作文，文長約120個單詞。文
分兩段，第一段描述兩張圖片中所呈現的場景，以及正在發生的狀況或
事件；第二段則敘述該事件(或故事)接下來的發展和結果。(109 年學測)

Many shopaholics look forward to the department stores' anniversary sales. Last year, I had the chance to join such an event with my mom. My mom was attracted by the advertisement and set her heart on a limited version brand-name bag. To make sure that we were "early birds," we hurried to the department store in the early morning. However, to our surprise, when we arrived, there had been a very long line! As soon as the door opened, people all rushed into the store, elbowing their way to get to the targets. I was not used to the rush and couldn't help but frown.

My mom and I finally managed to reach the bag shop with efforts. We nearly got suffocated by the crowds that left only little room for one another! We breathed a sigh of relief when we finished the shopping trip. This was the worst shopping experience I had ever had. What's worse, my mom found that the bag was stained. She hadn't noticed that because she had to shop in a rush with little time allowed for decision. Disappointed at the quality of the bag, my mom decided to ask for a refund. This made me frown again. I didn't want to do the shopping like fighting on a battlefield. I would like to be a wiser shopper who shops at leisure, carefully makes a shopping list and examines the quality of products. Impulse buying is the last thing I would do again!

說明：作者清楚描述圖片中所呈現的場景、敘述所發生的事件及後續發展，並在結尾提出想法加以說明。

〈參考範文 3〉

提示：請根據右方圖片的場景，描述整個事件發生的前因後果。文章請分兩段，第一段說明**之前**發生了什麼事情，並根據圖片內容描述**現在**的狀況；第二段請合理說明**接下來**可能會發生什麼事，或者**未來**該做些什麼。(98 年學測)

It seemed like another ordinary, silent night in this rural village. The diligent villagers, who had worked all day long, were all drifting off in their warm, cozy beds, not aware that a catastrophe was lurking in the dark.

All of a sudden, a meteorite shower hit! Enormous stones dived down one after another, bringing about horrible earthquakes. The villagers immediately awoke and strived to escape. The roar of the land, as well as the shrieking and crying of the people filled the air. Flames lit up the sky as the villagers made their way through collapsed houses—what a miserable sight!

The meteorites finally stopped falling, but it's just the beginning of more hardships. A man stood still, staring at his collapsed home and not knowing what to say. He was just the reflection of thousands of other suffering villagers. Yet after all, mere teardrops and grief wouldn't solve any problems. Villagers soon braced up and called for outside help and government support. They were convinced that with their perseverance, determination and positive actions, they would rebuild their homeland in the near future.

說明：98年學測英文考科中，史無前例地考對單張圖片前因後果的聯想。絕大多數的考生都敘述地震帶來災難，但是本文的作者別出心裁，描寫隕石撞擊地球，令人覺得耳目一新。本文用字貼切生動，並適當運用關係子句、分詞構句等句型。

◉ 〈參考範文 4〉

提示：下面兩本書是學校建議的暑假閱讀書籍，請依書名想想看該書的內容，
並思考你會選擇哪一本書閱讀，為什麼？請在第一段說明你會選哪一本
書及你認為該書的內容大概會是什麼，第二段提出你選擇該書的理由。

(104 年學測)

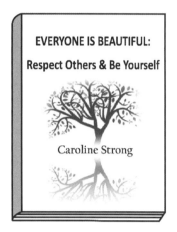

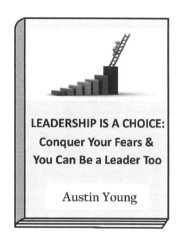

I would like to read the book *LEADERSHIP IS A CHOICE: Conquer Your Fears & You Can Be a Leader Too*. I suppose that the content of the book might be mainly about the life experiences of the fearless leaders. Moreover, I believe I could find some useful tips on how to conquer fears to be a good leader in this book.

I choose this book because I want to become a leader. Being quiet and shy, I admire those who are decisive and competent to direct a group of people. I hope that reading this book would cultivate my mind. I would put what is conveyed in the book into practice. In spite of the fears and nervousness that trouble me sometimes, I would follow the author's advice to conquer my inner fears and become a good leader too.

說明：作者觀察圖片並思考書名後，按照題目指示先在第一段說明自己所選的書並
推測書本內容，接著在第二段提出選擇該書的理由，藉此發表自己的想法。

◉ 〈參考範文 5〉

提示：下圖呈現的是美國某高中的全體學生每天進行各種活動的時間分配，請
　　　寫一篇至少120個單詞的英文作文。文分兩段，第一段描述該圖所呈現
　　　之特別現象；第二段請說明整體而言，你一天的時間分配與該高中全體
　　　學生的異同，並說明其理由。(103 年指考)

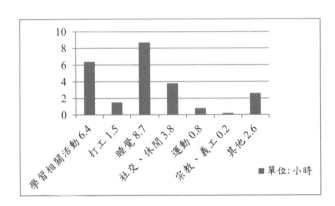

　　The bar chart shows how the students of an American high school manage their time. First of all, studying isn't the sole focus of their lives. They spend only around one-fourth of a day doing academic activities while they also get enough sleep, do exercise, and still have time to hang out or to socialize. What's more surprising to me is that they even have extra time to do part-time or voluntary jobs.

　　In contrast, my daily schedule is completely dominated by studying. Spending more than eight hours a day in school, I don't have much free time for hobbies or parties. What's worse, having enough sleep becomes a luxury to me, because heavy homework deprives me of just too much time. Cultural differences may be one of the key factors that contribute to the contrast. Different social values affect us and lead us to arrange our daily schedule accordingly. I wish someday, instead of being burdened with studying, I could manage my own time like those American high school students.

說明：這個作文題目要求判讀圖表並按照提示分段論述，寫作時應先看清楚該圖表
　　　所要表達的涵義，按照提示先在第一段說明此長條圖所代表的意義，並針對
　　　值得探討的「亮點」加以分析論述。接著第二段則比較自己在時間分配上與
　　　美國高中生相同或不同之處，並說明理由。

〈**Pictures for Exercise**〉

1. 提示：右圖為臺灣學生開始學英文的年齡。請根據此圖寫一篇文章。文章請分兩段，第一段描述圖表，第二段說明自己屬於哪一組，認為優缺點為何？

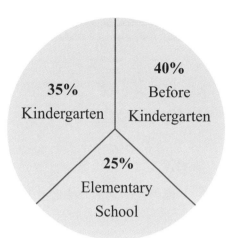

2. 提示：請根據下圖，描述車禍的前因後果。

3. 提示：請以下面編號1至4的四張圖畫內容為藍本，依序寫一篇文章，描述女孩與貓之間的故事。你也可以發揮想像力，自己選定一個順序，編寫故事。請注意，故事內容務必涵蓋四張圖意，力求情節完整、前後發展合理。(96 年學測)

III. 敘述文(Narration)

敘述文體通常要求同學敘述一個親身的經驗或事件。同學可以描述事件中的人、事、時、地、物等細節，來呈現事件的始末。在描述事件時，建議初學的同學採用順敘法。

〈參考範文 1〉

提示：指導別人學習讓他學會一件事物，或是得到別人的指導而自己學會一件事物，都是很好的經驗。請根據你過去幫助別人學習，或得到別人的指導而學會某件事的經驗，寫一篇至少120個單詞的英文作文。文分兩段，第一段說明該次經驗的緣由、內容和過程，第二段說明你對該次經驗的感想。(104 年指考)

　　In my neighborhood, I used to see an old couple walking hand in hand with happy smiles on their faces. However, I haven't seen the old man recently, and I could only see the old lady alone. I hesitated but finally asked her why. The old lady told me that the old man had passed away. Seeing the loneliness in her eyes, I decided to make a difference by teaching her how to surf the Internet through a smartphone step by step. At first, she considered it complicated and nearly dozed off. However, after a while, she found that it was fun to surf the Internet. What's more, she learned to contact her grandchildren abroad on Facebook. She thanked me with a warm smile that I had not seen for quite a while.

　　It was my first time plucking up the courage to start a conversation with a stranger. Even though the old lady had trouble remembering everything I taught her, we had a good time together. Besides, the more I demonstrated, the more interested she became, which made me feel content and delighted. In sum, helping others can also help me feel good.

說明：作者描述藉由教鄰居如何用手機上網來幫助其走出喪親之痛的經驗，先鋪陳這次經驗的緣由和過程，然後說明對於這次經驗的個人感想，理解到幫助別人能讓自己在心靈上也有所收穫及成長。

〈參考範文 2〉

提示：每個人從小到大都有覺得寂寞的時刻，也都各自有排解寂寞的經驗和方法。當你感到寂寞時，有什麼人、事或物可以陪伴你，為你排遣寂寞呢？請以此為主題，寫一篇英文作文，文長至少120個單詞。文分兩段，第一段說明你會因為什麼原因或在何種情境下感到寂寞，第二段描述某個人、事或物如何伴你度過寂寞時光。(106 年指考)

Growing up with three siblings, I had never felt lonely. We chatted, played, and fought together all the time. Yet, things changed when my siblings all left for college. Since then, I had often felt lonely when I got home. At school, I could chat and play with my classmates. However, when I was home, I had no one to play with or to fight with. In moments like this, I really missed my siblings.

Luckily, my lonely days ended before long. My parents brought me a small furry kitten. They told me that the kitten could be good company when my siblings were not home. I was touched and named the kitten Nana. From then on, this pet cat has taken the best part of my life. Now, the first thing I do after school is to play with Nana, and I enjoy her company when I am alone.

說明：本文敘述自己在何種情境下感到寂寞，並描述有貓咪相伴得以排遣寂寞時光。

〈**Topics for Exercise**〉

1. The Most Unforgettable/Embarrassing Experience

2. My Experience in Having a Part-Time Job/Learning English

3. An Unforgettable Trip/Experience/Class

4. A Bad Day/Misunderstanding

5. My Childhood

6. A(n) Bus/Train/Car/Taxi/Airplane Ride

7. A Family Reunion

8. One Thing That I Regret Most

IV. 描寫文(Description)

描寫文通常是要同學觀察人、事、物,並描述其外觀或自己的感受,可以描寫透過自己的感官所體會到的性質或狀態。如果是描寫地方,可以使用邏輯順序中的空間順序法。

◉ 〈參考範文〉

提示:你能想像一個沒有電(electricity)的世界嗎?請寫一篇文章,第一段描述我們的世界沒有了電以後,會是什麼樣子,第二段說明這樣的世界是好是壞,並舉例解釋原因。(96 年指考)

　　When I was asked to imagine a world without electricity, the time when a typhoon blacked out my neighborhood came into my mind. At first, it was troublesome for my family for we were unable to do the laundry, open the garage door to drive the car out, or simply have enough light to do my homework at night. As for myself, I became a bored living statue, just sitting there all day long for I had no TV to watch, no video games to play, and no Internet to surf. To sum up, it was a catastrophe made of total inconvenience and boredom.

　　But as I got used to this kind of lifestyle, things began to change. I started to save some water to wash my clothes by hand. I took a walk or rode a bike to school instead of taking my dad's car. TV, computer, and the Internet were all suddenly far away from my life. Ideas that I had never had flashed into my mind, and I started to write more things in my diary. I also spent more time playing with my pet dog. My life was without doubt more eco-friendly and refreshing. Now though we have already got back to the life with electricity, I sometimes miss that blackout period. To me, that silence had nothing to do with boredom, and the darkness couldn't be more enlightening.

說明:描寫停電時的生活,一開始覺得不方便,但是後來發現停電反而帶來沉澱心緒的優點。第二段的第一句是很好的轉承句,引領讀者文意將要轉換。

〈**Topics for Exercise**〉

1. A Restaurant I Like to Go to

2. A Visit to a Night Market/Museum/Library

3. My Favorite Scenic Spot in Taiwan

4. The City I Live in/I Like Best

5. The Person I Admire/Avoid Most

6. My Favorite Teacher/Festival/Sport/Movie/Book/Extracurricular Activity/Season

V. 說明文(Exposition)

1. 舉例法(Illustration/Providing Examples)

〈參考範文〉

提示：你認為家裡生活環境的維持應該是誰的責任？請寫一篇短文說明你的看
法。文分兩段，第一段說明你對家事該如何分工的看法及理由，第二段
舉例說明你家中家事分工的情形，並描述你自己做家事的經驗及感想。

(105 年學測)

　　In my opinion, maintaining a clean home is every family member's responsibility. A family functions well when everyone contributes to the home and takes on responsibilities. To begin with, family members can make a list of things to do together so as to share the household chores equally and effectively. By doing so, all members will be more involved and committed. In addition, parents can assign tasks to their children or allow them to choose the chores they prefer. Moreover, the family can have a discussion every now and then to see if anything needs to be adjusted.

　　Take my family for example. My parents make doing the household chores a regular routine. They believe that doing the chores helps build children's character. As a result, my brother and I have shared the chores since we were little. We started by doing small chores like putting toys away. Now, we have different chores, such as sweeping the floor and doing the laundry. To finish the chores and my homework in a limited time, I've also learned how to manage my time well. All in all, through doing the household chores, I'm delighted to help maintain a clean home and make myself a better person at the same time.

說明：在舉例類型的文章中，可以引用例子、細節、小故事或研究統計來使內容具
　　　體有說服力。

〈**Topics for Exercise**〉

1. Something Interesting About My Friend/Brother/Sister
2. A Bad Habit of Mine
3. Qualities of a Good Friend/Student/Child
4. My Favorite Taiwanese Delicacies

2. 提出理由法(Giving Reasons)

〈參考範文 1〉

提示：以下有兩項即將上市之新科技產品：

產品一：隱形披風
(invisibility cloak)

產品二：智慧型眼鏡
(smart glasses)

穿上後頓時隱形，旁人看不到你
的存在；同時，隱形披風會保護
你，讓你水火不侵。

具有掃描透視功能，戴上後即能
看到障礙物後方的生物；同時能
完整紀錄你所經歷過的場景。

　　如果你有機會獲贈其中一項產品，你會選擇哪一項？請以此為主題，寫一
篇至少120個單詞的英文作文。文分兩段，第一段說明你的選擇及理由，並舉
例說明你將如何使用這項產品。第二段說明你不選擇另一項產品的理由及該項
產品可能衍生的問題。(102 年指考)

　　If given a chance to choose one from the two technological products, I would choose the invisibility cloak. Using this cloak, I can keep myself from being seen whenever I am faced with bad guys. What's more, being both waterproof and fireproof, this cloak can protect me from any harm if I'm caught in flood or fire. Furthermore, I can also use this cloak to help those who are threatened by robberies or fire.

In comparison with the invisibility cloak, the smart glasses are less appealing to me. Since one of its two functions is to see through things, I'm worried that I may accidentally invade people's privacy. The other function of recording may trouble me as well. What if I don't want to recall all the bad things in life, but they have all been recorded? Due to these concerns, I prefer the invisibility cloak.

說明：作者依照提示，先在第一段說明個人選擇及理由，並舉例說明將如何使用這項產品，接著在第二段說明不選擇另一項產品的原因，以及該項產品可能衍生的問題。

〈參考範文 2〉

提示：請以運動為主題，寫一篇至少120個單詞的文章，說明你最常從事的運動是什麼。文分兩段，第一段描述這項運動如何進行 (如地點、活動方式、及可能需要的相關用品等)，第二段說明你從事這項運動的原因及這項運動對你生活的影響。(101 年指考)

Cycling is one of my favorite sports. It is suitable for most people, even of different ages and groups. To go cycling, in addition to the indispensable bicycle, a rider may need some sports gear, including a helmet to prevent harm to the head, gloves to keep hands comfortable, and sunglasses to protect eyes from the sun. Whoever feels like stretching the muscles can go cycling anytime and anywhere. What's more, this sport can be done by oneself or with others.

There are some reasons why I'm interested in cycling. First, it improves my fitness, refreshes my mind, and helps releasing my tension. Besides, I can enjoy beautiful views while cycling, particularly in the mountains. Moreover, I really enjoy going for a bicycle ride with my good friends. In a word, cycling benefits me mentally and physically.

說明：作者依照提示先在第一段描述進行這項運動的方式、需要的相關用品等，並在第二段列出這項運動帶來的好處及影響，以此說明從事這項運動的原因及理由。

〈Topics for Exercise〉

1. Why Money Isn't Everything

2. The Importance of Taking Exercise

3. Should Students Choose Their Own Hairstyle/Date/Bring Cellphones to School?

4. Why I Would Like to Be a Teacher/Doctor/Professor/Engineer

5. The Importance of Language Learning/Appearance/Self-Control/Health/Weight Control

6. The Importance of Time/Money Management

3. 定義法(Definition)

〈參考範文〉

What Is True Happiness?

Helping others brings me true happiness! Millions of people are suffering in the world, some from diseases, and some from poverty. That's why my parents have always encouraged me to participate in voluntary work since I was only ten. Sometimes I donate a little money or a few clothes to the poor. Sometimes I visit homeless people or orphans. I feel lucky because I am able to help those in need.

What's more, I find that many other Taiwanese feel the same way. For example, Lien Chia-En, a Taiwanese doctor, gave up his profitable career in Taiwan and devoted himself to helping the poor and the sick in Africa. Another good example is Master Cheng Yen, who founded the well-known charity organization "Tzu Chi" to help people in need across countries. In a word, Dr. Lien Chia-En and Master Cheng Yen, as well as I myself, find the happiness in our lives by reaching out a helping hand.

說明：定義法針對題目給予簡要明確的解釋，再據此來推展文句。使用定義法時第一句就要陳述定義，之後列舉細節或實例來說明。本篇文章開宗明義將快樂定義為幫助他人，再舉出其他例子說明其他人如何也在幫助他人時得到快樂。

〈**Topics for Exercise**〉

1. Humility

2. It Is Better to Give than to Receive

3. A Happy Global Villager

4. A True <u>Friend</u>/<u>Hero</u>/<u>Model Student</u>

5. What <u>Freedom</u>/<u>Independence</u>/<u>Happiness</u> Means to Me

6. An Ideal <u>Teacher</u>/<u>School</u>/<u>Parent</u>

7. The Hip-Hop Culture

4. 因果關係法(Cause and Effect)

因果關係類的文章有兩種，一是探討造成某事的原因，二是探討某事造成的影響。

〈**參考範文 1**〉

Why Are Some People Obsessed with Name-Brand Products?

Taipei 101, a hot spot located in a department-store-filled district of Taipei, is a place selling a great variety of fashion products. From vintage to modern, from casual to formal, only the sky is the limit of its diversity. However, behind all the differences they share one common thing: All of them are so-called "name-brand" products.

The fact raises the question of why so many people are obsessed with name-brand products. Some people say that they buy name-brand products just because these products that cost lots of money can cover up their true selves. That is, they have to rely on name-brand products to show their individuality. Others, on the other hand, hold a different opinion. To them, name-brand products are not about utility, but serve as items representing one's wealth, social status, and good personal taste. These two seemingly different explanations lead to one conclusion: People want to show themselves to be a particular type of people by using name-brand products.

說明：本文探討人們購買名牌產品的種種原因。

〈參考範文 2〉

The Effects of the Declining Birth Rate in Taiwan

Last month when I visited the elementary school I used to attend, the joyful sound of the kids brought me back to that 45-kids-filled classroom where I spent lots of good old days. But as soon as I stepped into the classroom again, a shocking image came into my eyes—there were only 28 seats, making the room rather spacious. It was not until then that I started to think about how the dropping birth rate might affect us as well as the society.

The most direct effect must be on the schools, because some of them will be forced to close due to the shortage of students, and this will cause the unemployment of many teachers and faculties. As these kids grow older, the lack of students turns into the lack of labors, resulting in the drop in the competitiveness of our country. What's more, with the advanced medical technology nowadays, people are living longer and longer. If the birth rate can not exceed the death rate, negative growth of the population will happen. To sum up, a lack of human resources and an aging society will be the main effects of the declining birth rate in Taiwan.

說明：本文探討低出生率從對學校到對社會造成的影響。

〈**Topics for Exercise**〉

1. How Global Warming Changed Our Climate
2. The Effects of the Internet/Globalization on My Life
3. The Importance of Good Sleep/a Balanced Diet
4. The Reasons Why Students Should Learn a Second Foreign Language

5. 過程分析法(Process Analysis)

用來說明做某件事的程序、步驟或方法。

〈參考範文〉

How to Get Along with Others

In the fast-paced society, the importance of knowing how to interact with people in harmony is undoubtedly self-evident. If everyone makes it to communicate well, we can avoid a lot of unnecessary conflicts and fights.

For me, I always treat others decently and heartily. First of all, I never jest or laugh at others, because I think it is boring and childish to make someone feel embarrassed. Second, I am a good listener. I always listen to people attentively and thoughtfully, showing great respect for others. Even when I hear something that I don't agree to, I won't just let out my disagreement immediately, but politely offer some opinions or advice. The most important of all, I empathize with others. Whenever I see someone suffering, I'll have an irresistible impulse to help them out without expecting anything in return. I have a dream that one day everyone can do exactly the same like me, and we are sure to transform the unbearable discord in our society into a harmonic symphony of love, care and fraternity!

說明：作者用first of all、second、the most important of all等轉承詞，很有條理
地提出與人相處的方法及步驟。

〈**Topics for Exercise**〉

1. How to Deal with Heavy Schoolwork/Pressure

2. How to Protect Our Environment

3. How to Stay Healthy and Smart

4. What Can We Do for Stray Animals?

5. What Should We Do When the Development of Modern Technology Threatens Our Environment?

6. 比較對照法(Comparison and Contrast)

比較法(comparison)是將兩樣事物作分析，比較兩者的相同點；而對照法(contrast)是對照兩者的不同點，一般用於相反或相對的情況。比較的方法有兩種：各邊呈現法(block organization)及特點呈現法(point-by-point organization)。可先把兩者的異同之處或者優缺點全部列出來，經過取捨後擬訂大綱，再依大綱發展文章。

〈範例題目〉The Advantages and Disadvantages of Being the Youngest Child in the Family

〈參考範文 1〉各邊呈現法(Block Organization)

Most people reckon that being the youngest child is lucky. However, as the youngest child in the family, I gradually realize the pros and cons of it. When it comes to the advantages, more tolerance from the family is the first thing thought of. If both elder and youngest child misbehave, it is highly possible to see the adults blame the elder for being "immature." On the contrary, the youngest child only received words like "mischievous." In addition, the experiences from elder brothers and sisters help smooth the rugged roads of the youngest child, allowing the youngest to have more chance to succeed.

Nevertheless, being the youngest child doesn't mean it's all smooth sailing. The first disadvantage is having no say in most things. For example, the youngest child seldom gets the upper hand in arguments with the elder. The second drawback is that the youngest child bears too many expectations from parents, and that really lays enormous pressure on the youngest child.

As the youngest child in the family, even if there is sometimes more pressure on my performance, I know it's for my own good and I appreciate the love from my family.

說明：本文採用各邊呈現法(block organization)，先談論身為最小的孩子的優點獲得較多容忍、人生旅途較順遂，然後再談論缺點為與兄姊吵架時常輸，並要承受較高的期待。

● 〈參考範文 2〉特點呈現法(Point-by-Point Organization)

Recently, many scientists have been arguing about how the birth order influences people, never coming to a conclusion. I myself am the youngest child in the family and I think there are some pros and cons of it.

First, parents are more seasoned when they bring up their youngest child, so the youngest child is usually better taken care of. But if the parents love their youngest one too much, he or she may be spoiled and behave improperly. Second, parents commonly love the youngest child more, so the youngest one usually has a happier childhood. Thus, the youngest child experiences less pressure from the family and is treated more liberally. However, this nurturing style may keep the youngest children from being independent of their parents and sometimes they count on their parents for everything, especially money.

To sum up, it is difficult to judge whether being the youngest child is good or not. However, if being the youngest, one should manage to not only cherish the advantages but also get rid of the disadvantages.

說明：特點呈現法(point-by-point organization)以要點為安排順序，提出要點如較成熟有經驗的父母、較多的關愛等，並在每一項要點下各自談論身為最小的孩子的優點及缺點。

〈**Topics for Exercise**〉

1. My Two Friends Are Similar/Different in Two Ways
2. Life in High School and Middle School
3. How Is Life Different for Men and Women?
4. The Advantages and Disadvantages of the Internet/Cellphones/Coeducation/ Wearing Uniforms/Watching TV/Modern Technology
5. What I Like and Dislike About My Life/School/Class/Personality
6. Should a College Student Live in a Dorm or at Home?

漢堡祕方 考前的提醒••

1. 用5W1H法則Who、What、When、Where、Why和How迅速找到文思。

2. 訂一個美味的大綱——吸引人的主題句、有趣的支持句、強而有力的結論句。

3. 段落裡的每個句子與主題密切相關；注意邏輯連貫性，並善用轉承詞及重複關鍵字。

4. 整個段落的時態及人稱要一致。

5. 善用漂亮的句型，如：分詞構句、倒裝句、強調句、感嘆句、假設語氣等。

6. 若能力及時間許可，可以將文章加長到約150–180字，以提高內容的分數。

7. 字跡清楚漂亮、內容好、文法錯誤少，必得高分。

••

Writing Exercise Sheet
寫作練習卷

提示：請參考本章的寫作範例，在下方標示的格線上練習寫一篇至少120個單詞的英文作文，可從本章提供的〈Topics for Exercise〉或〈Pictures for Exercise〉中挑選寫作題目，也可自訂題目，寫好後可利用下一頁所附的「寫作評估表」評估寫作成果。

Topic: _____ **Writer:** _____

_____

_____

_____

_____

_____

_____

_____

_____

_____

_____

_____

_____

_____

_____

_____

_____

_____

_____

_____

_____

_____

_____

Writing Evaluation Sheet
寫作評估表

請利用下表評估自己或同學的寫作成果。

Topic: _____ Writer: _____

Contents(內容)(5分)
Word Count(字數)
Topic Sentence(主題句)
Supporting Sentences(支持句)
Concluding Sentence(結論句)
Structure(組織)(5分)
Unity(統一性)
Coherence(連貫性)
Cohesiveness(緊密連接)
Appropriate Transitions or Linking Words(善用轉承詞)
Grammar & Sentence Patterns(文法及句構)(5分)
Avoiding Comma Splices, Run-On Sentences, or Sentence Fragments(正確斷句)
Subject-Verb Agreement(主詞、動詞在人稱及單複數上的一致)
Punctuation(正確使用標點符號)
Variable Sentence Patterns and Good Parallelism(句型富變化且平行結構確實對等)
Vocabulary & Spelling(字彙及拼字)(5分)
Diction(用字精確得宜)
Spelling(拼字正確)
Capitalization(大小寫正確)

Comments(評語)

Score: _____ Signature: _____

＊此份寫作評估表仿照大考配分，滿分為二十分，四大項目各占五分，各大項目下列出評分重點作為參考。若為方便計算課堂成績，亦可按比例將滿分調整為一百分，四大項目各占二十五分。可依課程需求作為部分項目評估，也可用來當作整體評估。

KEY
解答

Key 解答

☞ Chapter 2

Activity

1 *Topic sentence:*

Once my family and I went hiking at night.

Supporting sentences:

That was a beautiful evening and the moon was shining...My father talked to us about life.

Concluding sentence:

It was the most wonderful and unforgettable family activity to me.

2 *Topic sentence:*

On the Mid-Autumn Festival last year, my family and I went hiking at night to appreciate the beauty of the moon.

Supporting sentences:

We went to Elephant Hill near my house...What Father said that night has had a lifelong effect on me.

Concluding sentence:

This hiking trip has been the most impressive and meaningful family activity I have ever had.

☞ Chapter 3

Activity 1

Topic sentence:

Yearning to do something extraordinary while young, my classmates and I planned a bicycle tour around Taiwan this summer.

Supporting sentences:

We decided to travel around the island clockwise in twelve days...Meeting so

many friendly and hospitable people around the island was indeed heartwarming.
Concluding sentences:
Overall, I felt lucky to have joined this tour...and I will always cherish this amazing experience.

Chapter 4

Activity 1

1 The most unforgettable experience I had with my family happened last year, when my parents and I went to Mt. Ali to see the beautiful sunrise.
2 Whenever I recall the incident which happened two years ago, I regret not having done the right thing at the right time.

Activity 2

1 B; discussible   2 A; specific   3 B; specific   4 A; concise   5 B; active

Activity 3

1 c   2 b

Activity 4

(答案僅供參考)

1 If I had the ability to invent a new product, I would definitely invent a time machine.
2 The Internet greatly appeals to me mainly because of its online games.

Chapter 5

Activity 1

1 ade；f為結論句，bc無關主題   2 ace；f為結論句，bd無關主題

Activity 2

(答案僅供參考)

1 Powerful search engines on the Internet provide quick, useful and mostly free knowledge. They help us save great amounts of money, time, and energy when we look for information. Yet at the same time, the Internet also provides easy access to websites that contain violence or pornography. Therefore, users sometimes get addicted to the Internet and stop spending time reading or playing sports. It might do unimaginable harm to children and teenagers.

2 My parents and I always went to my grandparents' house in Keelung, where my grandma made rice dumplings. Inside the rice dumpling were my favorite egg yolk, peanuts, and chestnuts. It was so delicious that I would keep eating until I was told to stop. After lunch we would go watch different teams rowing dragon boats in the Keelung River. It was exciting to see those teams trying their best to grab the flag first and win the competition.

Activity 3

1 B，明確指出做了哪些菜。
2 A，舉出了數據來描述愛看電視的程度。
3 B，指出了明確的原因，而非概略的感受。
4 A，在名詞前後加上描述性的詞語，使句子更明確。

☞ Chapter 6

Activity 1

1 It is with courage and determination that Kevin makes the impossible possible and becomes a super hero in my heart.

2 Before I have enough money and time to really visit other countries, the Internet will always be my tour guide and a great channel to communicate with exotic cultures and foreign friends.

Activity 2

1 b   2 a

Activity 3

1 With a powerful leader and elaborate plans, Taiwan is sure to thrive again someday, restoring the honor of Formosa.

2 The experience taught me about the importance of life and I vowed that I would do everything carefully ever after.

☞ Chapter 7

Activity 1

第7句後離題，開始介紹學校及班級，沒有繼續敘述主題每天上學途中的匆忙。

Activity 2

1 Sometimes I try going jogging, too.

2 I am one of the best runners in my class.

3 I have great classmates in the class, including my best friend Jason.

Activity 3

1 空間順序──教室應配置有CD播放器、角落要有黑板及能投影在前方的投影機。

2 重要性順序──從最不重要列舉到最重要的特點：好的環境、有耐心的教師及有學習動機的學生。

3 時間順序──從幼稚園、小學、中學到大學的教室要有不同的功能及擺設。

Activity 4

1 1. As a result   2. However   3. then   4. As time went by   5. as soon as

2 1. therefore   2. First   3. Secondly   4. Lastly   5. In brief

3 1. In the past century   2. Unfortunately   3. As a consequence   4. Most important of all   5. In a word

Activity 5

1 B   2 A

Activity 6

a good English teacher, Such a teacher, he or she, this teacher, an ideal teacher, he or she, an ideal English teacher

Activity 7

既然主題句使用第三人稱，後面的句子也應一致使用第三人稱：they、their、they、they、their、Students。

☞ Chapter 8

Exercise 1

1. ...kindergarten because....
2. 正確
3. ...party. I have.... 或 ...party, for which I have....
4. ...hot. I.... 或 ...hot, so I....
5. ...unfair; therefore, ... 或 ...unfair. Therefore, ...
6. ...Leonard, who studied.... 或 ...Leonard. She studied....
7. ...two parts, a review....
8. ...healthy; moreover, ... 或 ...healthy. Moreover, ...
9. ...brilliant. It's.... 或 ...brilliant, and it's....
10. ...depression, fewer and fewer....

Exercise 2

1. ...difficult, as long as....
2. ...summer, the herbal doctor....
3. 正確
4. I was unable to....
5. 正確

6. shelter, <u>believes that</u>....

7. ...predicted, <u>the</u> climbers....

8. <u>I enjoy having</u>....

9. 正確

10. years, <u>they</u>....

Exercise 3

1. is；主詞為list　2. is；主詞為each　3. is；主詞為neither　4. is；主詞為a computer　5. am；動詞與I一致　6. are；data是datum的複數形　7. is；nine months視為一段時間　8. was；主詞為number　9. is；主詞為green tea，as well as grape seeds只是修飾語　10. is；spaghetti and meatballs為一道菜視為單數

Exercise 4

1. its；the Beatles為一個團體，為單數　2. me；between為介系詞，後面要接受格　3. their；analyses為analysis的複數形　4. my；my coming along作mind的受詞　5. whom；to為介系詞，其後要接受格　6. his or her；everybody為單數　7. he；as為連接詞，後面接主格　8. who；who為關係子句中sent動作的主詞　9. whom；whom作give the award to的受詞　10. who；who作will win the award的主詞

11. My Gucci dress, which I promised to lend my roommate, was not in the closet.

12. Carl said, "Nick, everyone in class is keeping his or her fingers crossed for you."

Exercise 5

1. Seeing her child off at the airport, <u>the mom burst into tears.</u> 或<u>When the mom was</u> seeing her child off at the airport, tears welled up in her eyes.

2. If lost, the ticket <u>cannot be replaced.</u>

3. When <u>I was</u> taking the school bus, it suddenly occurred to me that I forgot to bring my report which was due today. 或When taking the school bus, <u>I suddenly realized</u> that I forgot to bring my report which was due today.

4. To make a good bowl of beef noodles, <u>one needs</u> many ingredients to prepare the broth.

5. Because the radio <u>program</u> is broadcast at 6:30 a.m., Ian usually has time for <u>it</u> before school.

6. The two backpackers <u>carrying heavy luggage</u> decided to end their tour early.

7. My grandfather, <u>who is 70 years old now</u>, has spent 50 years doing research on the teaching of Confucius.

8. We expect to visit <u>in summer vacation</u> the town where Shakespeare was born.

9. The students complained that they <u>have barely</u> enough time to complete the assignments.

10. It was nice of Jackie to bring the sick bird <u>that he found in the woods</u> to the vet.

Exercise 6

1. ...better than <u>that of</u> Brownie.
2. ...a chapel, <u>a</u> water fountain, and a line of palm trees.
3. ...stood in line, bought their tickets, <u>and then ran</u> directly to....
4. ...<u>affected not only</u> the students but also the teachers.
5. ...is equal to <u>Eliza's</u>.
6. The children always have <u>remembered</u> and always will remember....
7. Harry was cold, tired, and <u>hungry</u>.
8. ...that my parents love me more than <u>Monica does</u>. 或 ...that my parents love me more than <u>they love Monica</u>.
9. I <u>know neither</u>....
10. Living in Tokyo is as expensive <u>as</u>, ...

Exercise 7

1. " " ? 2. — 3. " " 4. , " , " 5. — — 6. : 7. : 或 , 8. : 9. — —
10. ! " " " . "

Exercise 8

1. There is a stray cat meowing at the door.
2. There are eight males and five females in the committee.
3. Five typhoons hit Taiwan that year.
4. Two students dropped out this semester.

Exercise 9

1. cost 2. took 3. cost 4. spent 5. spent 6. took 7. cost 8. takes
9. spent

Exercise 10

1. rise 2. risen 3. Raise 4. raise 5. arise 6. rose 7. rose 8. raising 9. rise
10. raised

Exercise 11

1. sometime 2. some time 3. some times 4. Sometimes

Exercise 12

1. lie 2. lays 3. laid 4. lied 5. lies 6. lied

Exercise 13

1. few 2. less 3. fewest 4. little 5. fewer 6. least

Exercise 14

1. Every day 2. everyday

Exercise 15

1. is used to 2. is used to 3. used to

Exercise 16

1. hard 2. hardly 3. hard

Exercise 17

1. may be 2. Maybe

Exercise 18

1. 正確   2. badly→bad   3. sweetly→sweet   4. happily→happy   5. 正確
6. confidently→confident   7. good→well   8. well→good   9. fastly→fast
10. sudden→suddenly

Exercise 19

1. as   2. like   3. like   4. as

掌握關鍵，瞄準致勝！

學測指考英文
致勝句型

王隆興／編著

致勝關鍵

關鍵1 **名師嚴選80個句型重點！**
完整收錄大考常見句型，並比較易混淆的句型，清楚掌握重點，舉一反三。

關鍵2 **解說清楚明瞭一看就懂！**
重點一目瞭然，說明淺顯易懂好吸收，考前衝刺神隊友，迅速提升考場即戰力。

關鍵3 **隨堂評量實戰練習現學現用！**
隨書附贈20回隨堂評量，及時檢視學習成果、熟悉句型，以收事半功倍之效。

國家圖書館出版品預行編目資料

漢堡式大考英文段落寫作 Paragraph Writing: Easy as
a Hamburger／林君美編著. －－二版二刷. －－臺北
市：三民，2024
　　面；　公分. －－(英語Make Me High系列)

ISBN 978-957-14-6823-5　(平裝)

1. 英語 2. 作文 3. 寫作法

805.17　　　　　　　　　　　109006640

英語 Make Me High 系列

漢堡式大考英文段落寫作　Paragraph Writing: Easy as a Hamburger

編 著 者	林君美
創 辦 人	劉振強
發 行 人	劉仲傑
出 版 者	三民書局股份有限公司 (成立於 1953 年)

三民網路書店
https://www.sanmin.com.tw

地　　　址	臺北市復興北路 386 號　　　(復北門市)　(02)2500-6600
	臺北市重慶南路一段 61 號 (重南門市)　(02)2361-7511
出版日期	初版一刷 2009 年 5 月
	二版一刷 2021 年 11 月
	二版二刷 2024 年 7 月
書籍編號	S808080
I S B N	978-957-14-6823-5

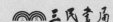